The Raven League

Sherlock Holmes is Missing!

The Raven League:

Sherlock Holmes is Missing!

by
Alex Simmons and Bill McCay

The Raven League: Sherlock Holmes is Missing!

RAZORBILL/SLEUTH

Published by the Penguin Group
Penguin Young Readers Group
345 Hudson Street, New York, New York 10014, U.S.A.
Penguin Group (USA) Inc., 375 Hudson Street,
New York, New York 10014, U.S.A.
Penguin Group (Canada), 90 Eglinton Avenue, Suite 700,
Toronto, Ontario, Canada M4P 2Y3 (a division of Pearson Penguin Canada Inc.)
Penguin Books Ltd, 80 Strand, London WC2R 0RL, England
Penguin Ireland, 25 St Stephen's Green, Dublin 2,
Ireland (a division of Penguin Books Ltd)
Penguin Group (Australia), 250 Camberwell Road,
Camberwell, Victoria 3124, Australia
(a division of Pearson Australia Group Pty Ltd)
Penguin Books India Pvt Ltd, 11 Community Centre,
Panchsheel Park, New Delhi – 110 017, India
Penguin Group (NZ), Cnr Airborne and Rosedale Roads,
Albany, Auckland 1310, New Zealand (a division of Pearson New Zealand Ltd)
Penguin Books (South Africa) (Pty) Ltd, 24 Sturdee Avenue, Rosebank,
Johannesburg 2196, South Africa

Penguin Books Ltd, Registered Offices: 80 Strand, London WC2R 0RL, England

10 9 8 7 6 5 4 3 2 1

Library of Congress Cataloging-in-Publication Data is available

Printed in the United States of America

Chapter

"COME ON, FIGHT!" NAT BLOUNT JEERED. "OR ARE you yellow? Is that why you let poor Tim Doolan down?"

Archie Wiggins slowly pulled himself up from the grimy cobblestone pavement. His ribs ached where Nat had just kicked him.

"Tim got killed, and you done nothing. Well, we ain't going to take that." Blount was talking to his audience now—the other four boys in a half circle around them. They were faceless blurs to Wiggins. With the skin around one eye swollen and bleeding, he could barely make out Nat.

The windowless walls of the crooked little alley seemed to close in as Nat came at him again. Wiggins brought up his fists, still trying to understand how the rot had spread—and how deeply Nat Blount had spread it. Now it was "poor Tim Doolan." But when the boy was alive, Nat had mocked him as "that Irish ape."

They shuffled back and forth, Wiggins blocking Blount's fists. "Not as easy as thieving," Wiggins panted, "eh, Natty lad?"

Blount's skinny face went red, his lips pulling back from snaggled yellow teeth until he looked like the rat he was. He hated that nickname because it was also slang for a pickpocket. That's what Nat had been before Wiggins brought him into the Irregulars—and probably what Nat still did when he got off on his own. The Baker Street Irregulars were supposed to be Mr. Sherlock Holmes's eyes and ears on the streets. Under Wiggins, they'd done good work for the great detective and gotten good pay. But that was then . . .

When Tim was murdered, Wiggins knew he should have gone to Holmes for help, but he didn't dare talk to the detective. Those cold eyes were too good at digging out the truth, and Wiggins couldn't face that.

Nat got past Wiggins's defense, hammering in with a left and a right. Wiggins tottered back, dropping to his knees. Most times, he'd have landed in an inch or two of mud. But the London summer weather had been fair the last five weeks, so he only stirred up a cloud of gritty dust.

Weak and dizzy, Wiggins tried to get back to his feet, to raise his arms. But pain and a horrible sick feeling blocked his brain's desperate commands to his body.

"Now, *Archibald Francis* Wiggins." Blount practically spat out every syllable of Wiggins's full name. "Here's the end of your precious Baker Street Irregulars—and of you."

All Wiggins could do was watch blurrily as Nat Blount reared back for a kick that would crack teeth or ribs. The rest of the boys gathered round.

But the blow never came.

The Irregulars froze at the clatter of running feet coming around the bend in the alley, turning guilty looks toward the stranger who suddenly appeared. All their pale skins had a grimy grayness, thanks to the soot sifting down from a million London chimneys. But this boy's skin was darker. The ash showed whitish against the warm brown of his complexion.

Wiggins shook his head, still trying to clear his vision. He'd seen this boy before, running errands around the East End. What was his name—Evans? No, Owens, they called him.

One of the Irregulars stepped into Owens's path. "G'wan, golliwog," he said. "Don't go stickin' yer black nose where it ain't wanted."

For a second, Owens's face clenched as tight as his fists. Then, looking at Nat, the four other boys, and Wiggins on his knees, he deliberately relaxed himself and shrugged. "Your business is your business," Owens said. "Mine is getting away from the blueboy who's chasin' me."

"A copper?" Nat Blount looked from his skinned knuckles to Wiggins's face.

At the mention of police, the others ran off and disappeared down the other end of the alley. Nat, however, moved to peer back the way Owens had come. "I don't see any cop—"

He got no further as Owens's fist crashed into the side of his head. The boy's eyes rolled up, and a second later he lay stretched out on the cobblestones.

"Fool's punch," Owens muttered, wringing his hand. "Hurts almost as much to give as to receive." He turned to Wiggins. "Up, you."

"Wha—why?" It hurt to speak, and he felt a salty, coppery taste in his mouth. "Why are—"

"Because there ain't no copper coming." Owens hauled Wiggins to his feet. "So we'd best be away before those lads come back."

They reached the street, where Wiggins shook off Owens's supporting arm. "I mean, why did you help?"

"For one thing, I ain't nobody's golliwog." Owens's lips twisted as if he were about to spit. "For another, I don't like five-against-one odds." He switched moods, suddenly grinning. "Of course, that one fella seemed more than enough for you."

Wiggins tried to bluster. "I was—"

"Wearing out his fist with that Irish snout of yours."

Wiggins touched his nose and winced. He glared at Owens. "I ain't no bleedin' Irishman."

The other boy shook his head. "No, you're just bleedin'. You think you'll be able to go off on your own?"

One step and Wiggins found himself staggering. His ribs ached something fierce. Owens caught him by the arm. "Where do you live?"

Wiggins told him, and they set off together. "Have to clean meself up before Mam sees me," he mumbled.

"You're lucky your clothes didn't get torn up," Owens said.

Wiggins's trousers were nothing to get excited about. They were far too big for him: the cuffs rolled up several times, the waist coming halfway up his chest, where it was held in place by a piece of twine acting as a belt. His shirt, however, fit better and was made of good cotton, mended in only a couple of places.

Now he wiped ineffectually at some dirty spots. "Guess Nat was more interested in my face," Wiggins said. He caught his reflection in a shop window and grimaced. That brought a whole new set of pains. His lip was split, and the skin on his right cheek and around his eye was beginning to puff up.

"We might be able to get some help here." Owens led them through the door to what had once been the front parlor of an old house. A striped pole by the door advertised a barbershop. "Mr. Shears?"

"Shears by name, a shearer by profession," replied a skinny little man, bald-headed with a pair of long, bushy sideburns. "Why, it's young Owens! How are you, my boy?"

"Well enough, sir," Owens replied. "My friend here could use some help."

The barber frowned as he looked at Wiggins. "Been in a fight, eh? And not, I think, on the winning side."

"At least he didn't knock any teeth out," Wiggins admitted gloomily as Owens helped him into a chair.

"Mr. Shears took care of my father. Dad was the boxing champion of his regiment." Owens's dark brown eyes glowed with pride.

"*Corporal* Shears I was then, and I wouldn't have this shop today without some bets I made on Tommy Owens." The barber used a damp towel to clean the crusting blood from Wiggins's face. Then he dabbed something that tasted like poison and burned like a hot poker onto the cut on Wiggins's lip. While Wiggins sputtered, Shears ran careful fingers across the boy's face. "Nothing broken, but we'll have to do something about that swelling near your right eye."

Wiggins stared at Owens. "Your old man was in the army?" he asked in surprise. "I didn't think they had any—"

"My dad was white," Owens replied. "He and my mother met in the Islands. They married, and he brought her back here." Owens stared out the grimy shop window. "That worked out real well."

"Things would be different if your dad were still with us," Shears told Owens. Reaching for a shelf, the barber brought down a jar and carefully fished out what looked like a fat-bodied worm.

"Here, now," Wiggins yelped in alarm.

"It's either a leech or a lot of pain and having that eye turn all the colors in creation," Shears warned.

Wiggins tensed as the man approached him with the squirming, bloodsucking creature. He wasn't exactly mad about having the wriggling thing planted on his cheek. But by the time Shears dabbed the creature with vinegar to make it fall off, the swelling had gone down, and his face didn't hurt as much. In fact, Wiggins felt almost normal—until he tried to get out of the barber's chair. He held his middle, wincing.

"Cold compresses tonight," Shears advised, "or you'll be walking about like an old man tomorrow."

"What do I owe you?" Wiggins asked, reaching into his pocket. He'd earned a few pence running errands with the Irregulars that morning. The money should go to help pay the rent on the rooms where he and his mother lived, but a debt was a debt.

Shears surprised him by shaking his head. "No charge for a friend of young master Owens."

Wiggins glanced at the other boy, who only shrugged.

"You have any jobs as need doing—*any*—I'm your lad." Wiggins went to the door carefully, followed by Owens.

"You still need help getting—"

"No." Wiggins's answer popped out all too quickly. He stared at the uneven cobblestones under his bare feet. "I suppose I should thank you," he said gruffly.

"Don't choke tryin' to get the words out."

Wiggins's eyes jerked up. Owens's face was as tight as the first time Wiggins saw him in the alley, facing down Nat and the others—saving someone he didn't even know.

"It's just—I ain't used to getting help from anyone, specially for no reason," Wiggins said. "I won't forget that, Owens."

Owens blew on his skinned knuckles. "I'll remember too." He nodded, then quickly turned and went on his way.

Wiggins set off for home. At first he had to take

careful steps, but soon he moved more normally as sore muscles stretched.

His parting words with Owens kept echoing in his head. Well, it would be hard to forget one of the worst days of his life. Blount had destroyed the Baker Street Irregulars, and that hurt Wiggins even more than the beating.

He moved east on Whitechapel Road, a wider street that was clogged with traffic. Besides wagons and horse-drawn buses, people jammed the sidewalks. The East End of London was a crowded as well as a poor section of town. Street merchants hawked their merchandise at the top of their voices. Women, the ones with money at least, were hurrying home from shopping. Men were heading home from work or to their local pubs for a drink. Others were heading west to the more prosperous parts of the city, hoping to earn or beg a little money from the posh folk at restaurants, theaters, or concert halls. He and Tim had spent many an evening that way while also keeping an eye out for any business that might interest Sherlock Holmes.

Images flashed across Wiggins's mind. It was a dank, foggy night, not too many weeks ago, but much later than it was now. The theater crowd was letting out, the fancy patrons all decked out in their sparkling jewels and shining silk hats. Their pockets and stomachs were full, unlike his and Tim's. Then they saw . . .

The image ceased as if some dark door had slammed shut. *Not now.* He jammed suddenly shaky hands into his pockets, hearing the unspoken accusations of the Irregulars. *You're a coward. That's why Tim is dead.*

And maybe it's true, he thought.

Hemmed in by the crowd around him, Wiggins felt alone. Thieving Nat Blount had stolen the best thing in Wiggins's life, along with all the lads Wiggins had believed were his friends. Even worse, his one true friend had been stolen weeks before—murdered.

Wiggins knew he should go to Mr. Holmes and tell all, but he stumbled just at the thought of it. So Tim's death would remain a mystery because the events of that night had not only taken Tim Dolan but also Archie Wiggins's courage.

Chapter 2

AT THE END OF WHITECHAPEL ROAD, WIGGINS turned off onto a narrower street. Buildings hereabouts seemed to sag under the weight of too many people, too many years of neglect, too much dirt.

For Wiggins, this was home. He made his way through the maze of side streets, cutting through a tunnel-like passage to reach the crooked lane where he lived.

Though it was late in the afternoon, Wiggins found a strange energy in the air. Neighborhood shopkeepers and patrons seemed livelier going about their work or chores. Had he felt better, Wiggins might have tried to find out what the excitement was about, but the soreness in his muscles told him to press on home.

He was surprised to find his mother waiting

outside the grimy brick building where they lived with six other families. "There you are," she said, hurrying him to the water tap in the backyard. "Wash yourself and try to do something about your hair. Then go and put on your boots."

"Do I have to?" Wiggins complained.

The boots had belonged to his father, dead now for five years. They didn't really fit, and Wiggins had to stuff them with rags and newspaper. He preferred going barefoot, especially in the summertime.

"We're having company, and you *will* look your best." His mother darted back into the kitchen. Wiggins caught the smell of baking. Every night, she got up hours before sunrise, baking bread and cakes. Some days they lived on stale items that hadn't sold. She never baked in the afternoon. Whoever was coming must be very important.

Wiggins tried unsuccessfully to get the spikes of reddish brown hair to lie flat, then went to the room he shared with his mother. She had carefully swept the place and had somehow found flowers to put in the chipped washing pitcher. He just finished tying the laces on his boots when his mother appeared in the doorway. She looked nervous.

"Clara Stanley was my best friend back home in Tollton. She married Allen James, who had the biggest farm in the area, and I married your father."

Wiggins nodded. He knew the rest of the story. His father had been an engineer, handy with all sorts of machinery. He'd come to London hoping to make better wages. Instead, he'd worked long and hard until his heart gave out. Now his widow worked even harder but wasn't eager to marry again, saying Wiggins's pa was a hard man to replace.

"The place looks nice, Mam," Wiggins said.

His mother whisked off her apron. "It's been years since I heard from Clara. She doesn't know about your father. They should be here any minute."

Wiggins was a bit confused when the door opened ten minutes later. Their visitors were not a husband and wife, but a mother and daughter. Clara James was a faded blond woman who had once been pretty. Now she seemed thin and sick, with dark patches under her eyes. Her daughter, Eugenia, was a tall fair-haired girl about Wiggins's age. She wore a nice blouse and skirt—a skirt that had recently been lengthened. The new material didn't quite match.

The moment she came into the room, the girl looked around. Wiggins was uncomfortably aware of her eyes taking in the single chair, the chip missing from the pitcher, the faint bloody smudges on his shirt that Mr. Shears and Owens hadn't quite been able to clean away.

"We spent weeks looking for you," Mrs. James said, "ever since leaving Tollton. Allen died back in March, and his cousin inherited the farm. We couldn't stay, and . . . well, I hoped that you and Robert—" She faltered at the look on Mam's face, taking in the room for the first time.

"Son," Mrs. Wiggins said quietly, "perhaps you and Eugenia might go outside for a bit."

"Please, ma'am, call me Jennie," the girl said. "You too, Archibald."

He winced at hearing his proper name. "Everyone calls me Wiggins."

Both exchanged looks, each unwilling to be saddled with the other. But staying there with the grown-ups was even more uncomfortable.

They left the house in silence. Outside in the street, however, the girl spoke up. "I think you're lucky that we came today. Otherwise your mother would have more to say about you getting into a fight." She gave him a superior smile. "And from the look of it, you didn't win."

A fruit-and-vegetable hawker came past, a little donkey pulling his barrow. "Oh, blast." Jennie twitched her skirt away from the cloud of dust that followed them. "Of all the filth—"

That was the last straw. "Maybe I got some spatters on me, missy," Wiggins burst out. "It comes from living in the nastiest, dirtiest part of London. At least I don't put on airs."

Jennie's face went bright red under the sprinkle of freckles across her nose and cheeks. "I'm not!" she protested. "It's not putting on airs, trying to look respectable."

Wiggins grinned unpleasantly. "How many dresses did you pick apart to make that skirt?"

Jennie's eyes blazed. "Did you ask your father if you could wear his shoes?"

"I would have," Wiggins shot back, "if he were alive!"

They were quiet for a moment, each aware a line had been crossed. "I'm sorry," Jennie said finally. "We have little enough since we came to London. It's an expensive place." She looked down. "I think my mother hoped to ask your family for help."

"Hard enough to keep our own heads above water," Wiggins admitted. "Things were well enough when I was little, but work started getting scarce for my dad. Then he died, and my younger brother followed on soon after that."

"How?" Jennie asked.

"Fever." Wiggins's bitter gaze took in the worn buildings around them, the half-starved neighbors, the piles of trash scattered about the streets. "It's best not to get sick round here. Doctors are expensive."

Jennie lowered her head but said nothing.

"Now it's just Mam and me," Wiggins continued. "She bakes, and I do what I can."

"We've been sewing flags so people can wave them for the Queen's Golden Jubilee next week."

"Oh, that." Wiggins smiled sourly. Now he understood the reason for the neighborhood's excited mood. "Don't suppose they pay for them flags in gold."

"We get paid in pennies," Jennie said. "They call it the Golden Jubilee because Queen Victoria has been on the throne for fifty years."

"Hoy! Wiggins!" a loud young voice broke in. "There's no dodging me this time!"

Wiggins spun round, expecting to find an angry Irregular coming after him. Instead, he saw a boy who barely came up to his chest.

"Dooley." Wiggins groaned. The last thing in the world he wanted was a chat with Tim Doolan's younger brother, especially in front of Jennie.

"Why d'you keep running off whenever I try to talk to you about Tim?" Dooley banged down the large wooden shoe shine box he carried at Wiggins's feet, shook back a mass of red curls from his eyes, and glared. "You've done nothing about Tim being killed," Dooley accused. "Why?"

"You don't know what I been doing," Wiggins shot back.

"I do." The young boy tapped a finger painfully into Wiggins's bruised chest. "*Nothing!* Nat and the others told me how you haven't gone to Sherlock Holmes, and—"

"Sherlock Holmes?" Jennie broke in. "The detective?"

Dooley ignored the interruption. "Tim told me what you did for Mr. Holmes, keeping an eye out for suspicious things and all. Since you weren't doing nothing, I decided to talk to your guv'nor myself. I went to Baker Street this morning—"

"*What?*" Wiggins couldn't say any more. The words seemed frozen in a solid clump from his chest to his stomach.

If Dooley told Mr. Holmes about Tim, the detective would soon be summoning Wiggins, questioning him. . . .

"But he wasn't there," Dooley grumbled. "The old bat at the door just about had the coppers on me. Still, I hung about, figuring I'd recognize him even if I'd never set eyes on him before. As it turns out, I got on better with the serving girl who swept the walk." He ran a hand through his wild red curls. "We got the same color hair."

His expression got more serious. "She said that he'd been away almost a week, and they expected him back two days ago. Then there's what I found out on Repton Street."

"Half the scum in the British Empire washes up there!" Wiggins burst out. "Smugglers, cut-throats—"

"That's where the bad'uns would have taken Tim, the way I figured it," Dooley said. "They're always heavin' someone in the river round there."

"You could have been one of them!" Wiggins growled.

"I was smart," Dooley insisted. "Had me shoe shine kit and me eyes—and ears—open. This afternoon I saw two hard characters carrying a rug into one of the boardinghouses. It looked a lot heavier than you'd expect. So I followed 'em."

Wiggins's mouth hung open in disbelief.

Dooley gave a smug nod. "Kidnappers," he declared.

"Why do you think that?" Jennie asked.

Wiggins shot her a look. This was all he needed—some girl taking an interest in his business.

"'How many people bring a rug into a place where you just rent a bed?'' I asked myself," Dooley said to Jennie. "So I nipped round to the back alley to see what I could see."

"And what was that?" Jennie asked.

"They came into a room, but they weren't carrying a rug anymore. It was a long geezer instead."

"A person?" Wiggins shrugged. "Maybe they were just shifting someone out of a bed—a drunk."

"What do you mean by long?" Jennie asked.

"I only saw legs," Dooley said. "*Long* legs. This bloke had to be taller than my dad. And they were tied together at the ankles." He shot a challenging glance at Wiggins. "You don't do that with no drunk."

"Maybe it's someone who owes them money," Wiggins said. "Could be they just want to teach him a lesson."

"Not from what I heard 'em say." Dooley leaned toward Wiggins. "One told the other, 'We should just wait for a good fog and dump 'im in the river—like I done with the other one.'"

Dooley gazed at Wiggins with a terrible intensity. "That's how it was when Tim died, wasn't it? It was a foggy night, a real London Particular—right?"

"I think—" Wiggins broke off, trying not to let the unease he felt show. "You shouldn't expect that those blokes had anything to do with Tim. It's like you said—lots of folks wind up in the river."

"They do?" Jennie asked, her voice squeaky with shock.

Good, Wiggins thought. *Maybe that idea will keep her from poking her freckled nose in where it isn't wanted.*

Dooley's eyes narrowed. "There's more. First the kidnappers looked out the window a few times, so I dropped down and took a walk round the block. When I came back, the room looked empty. So I climbed up for a closer look. It *was* empty, so I went in."

"You broke into a Repton Street lodging house?" Wiggins exploded. "You're lucky someone didn't slit your—"

"The important thing is, I found a clue." Dooley reached into his shirt and held up his prize. It was a woolen tweed hat with visors in front and back—a deerstalker cap.

"Maybe now you'll believe me," he told Wiggins. "When those fellas were talking about fog and dumping somebody in the Thames—that had to be Tim. And this—" Dooley shoved the cap in Wiggins's face. "I only know one long geezer who goes around wearing one of these, and that's Mr. Sherlock Holmes! Well, now I know why he ain't home. He's gone and got himself kidnapped!"

Chapter

Dooley's eyes flashed with excitement as he flapped the cap around. "You've been as close to Mr. Holmes as I am to you. I bet you've even seen this hat on his head."

Wiggins grabbed hold of the cap. It did look familiar, but . . .

"Mr. Holmes ain't the only bloke in London who sports a deerstalker," he said.

"You know I'm right!" Dooley snatched back the hat.

For a moment, Wiggins stood in silence. He hadn't been able to face Holmes, and so Tim's death went unsolved. Now Dooley was out playing detective, and that just wasn't safe.

"I'll tell you what *I* know," Wiggins finally said. "Whoever had that room was probably a nasty piece of work, and you just nicked a hat from him. Better hope he or his friends don't spot you with it. Or saw you do it."

"I know what I saw," Dooley insisted, waving around the cap. "Why don't you call out the Irregulars? Let them look for those—"

"'Cause—'cause this ain't none of our business," Wiggins lied. How could he tell Dooley that the Irregulars were no more? He found it hard to believe himself.

"Maybe you don't care about nobody no more, or—" Dooley crossed his arms over his chest. "Are you afraid?"

"I ain't afraid of nothing! Don't you ever say that to me! *Ever!*" Wiggins grabbed Dooley and shook him.

Jennie caught hold of Wiggins's arm, and Wiggins released the younger boy. He pushed off Jennie's hand and stared down at the ground.

"If someone is in trouble, shouldn't we tell the police?" Jennie asked.

Wiggins forced back a shudder, remembering that foggy night and a sneering figure in blue. He made himself meet Jennie's eyes. "Maybe where you came from, the coppers all tip their hats and say, 'Righto, Miss Eugenia, we'll get on it sharpish!' East End blueboys got a different attitude." His voice grew bitter.

"They don't care what happens to anyone down here."

"I don't believe that." Jennie's face was so pale, the spray of freckles across her cheeks and nose stood out.

"You will," Dooley told her.

"Even if you're right," Jennie went on, "wouldn't they care if they knew it was Mr. Holmes?" She pointed to the deerstalker in Dooley's hands. "If we could prove it?"

"And how would we do that, ma'am?" Wiggins inquired sarcastically.

"I know a tailor boy and his family near to where we live," Jennie said. "They know all about clothes and things."

"Maybe they could tell us who made the hat and who bought it!" Dooley exclaimed.

"You're daft!" Wiggins glared at them, realizing nothing he could say would stop them. "Fine!" he shouted. "You two go waste your time. I've got to earn something today, and it's getting late. Rent day is coming. And unlike some I know, Mam and I can't depend on other folk to help us."

Jennie went red and Wiggins felt a brief pang that perhaps he'd gone too far.

"I'll be doing some chores at the Raven Pub," Wiggins said. "Dooley knows where it is. You two can come there when you finish chasing wild geese!"

Even as he stomped off, his anger melted away. *Dooley was right*, he thought miserably. *I* am *afraid*. Suddenly he felt as if this weren't the familiar East End, but a dark hallway where he was walking into unknown danger. A hallway just like the one he'd run through that terrible night.

Jennie saw Dooley glance back as they walked away from Wiggins. "I don't know what's the matter with Wiggins," he said in a puzzled voice. "He ain't usually like that."

"You couldn't prove it by me," Jennie replied. But then she realized that she wasn't acting like her usual self either. Why was she even on this errand? She'd just met Wiggins and had no connection to Dooley. So why had she agreed to accompany him?

Perhaps it was because her usual life had grown worse and worse these last few months. With her father's death, Jennie's uncle took over the family farm—that was the law. Jennie and her mother quickly learned there was no room for them anymore. Since coming to London, their lives seemed to move in ever-decreasing circles—as if they were being sucked down a sewer drain. If she didn't find help and soon, things would become much worse. Wiggins, Dooley—and Sherlock Holmes—offered the first chance to improve her situation that she had found since coming to the city. Jennie intended to cling to them the way a drowning sailor clings to a piece of floating wreckage.

If Dooley noticed her silence, he didn't mention it. He chattered about the best places to set up his shoe shine box and ply his trade. Jennie stopped in front of a small storefront that had been cut into two even tinier shops. The door and window frame had dingy, peeling paint. But the window itself was spotlessly clean, the card in one pane neatly lettered.

"Geismar Tailors," Jennie read aloud. "This is it."

Dooley gave her a sidelong look. "So these would be Jewish folk?"

"Yes," she replied. "So?"

He shrugged. "We don't usually have much to do with them, except for a bit of buying and selling They're different, ain't they?"

Back home and even here in London, Jennie had heard plenty of people making worse remarks about "Irish folk." But she wasn't going to say that to Dooley.

"They may give my mother and me some work," Jennie said. "Not to mention some information for *us*." She walked into the shop.

Inside, a slender boy walked up to her. He was about Wiggins's age but otherwise his complete opposite. The boy wore a clean white shirt with a collar. His brown hair was neatly parted down the center, his dark trousers were without stains or patches, and he wore shoes. Jennie glanced beyond him to the back of the shop, where two women sat at sewing machines—the boy's mother and sister.

"Hello, Jennie," he said politely.

"This is Jacob Geismar," Jennie said to Dooley. "His family moved here about a year ago. Jacob, this is Doo—"

"William Doolan," the young boy declared formally. Then he grinned. "But everyone calls me Dooley."

"We need your help, Jacob," Jennie said. Dooley held out the deerstalker. "Can you tell us anything about this hat?"

"We think it belongs to Sherlock Holmes," Dooley added. "And we think he's in trouble."

Jennie explained how they had come by the hat.

Jacob stared at Dooley. "You broke into someone's room and took this?"

"He saw a person in that room being held prisoner," Jennie pointed out. "And if that person was Mr. Holmes, we have to tell the police. But they won't believe us without proof."

Jacob took the cap. "Let me ask my father."

He called to the back of the store and a man stepped out from behind a curtain. He was an older version of Jacob except he was taller, stooped from long hours of sewing, and had thinning hair. His gaze locked on Dooley. It wasn't a friendly look.

For an instant, Jennie saw herself and Dooley through the man's eyes, remembering a phrase she'd read in newspaper stories about London. "Street Arabs," that's what the writers had called the city's thieving, unsupervised, poor children.

Taking her courage in both hands, Jennie smiled at Mr. Geismar. "My friend found this nearby. We were hoping you might help us return it to its proper owner."

The shop owner's glance at Dooley suggested he didn't believe the boy had "found" anything. Grumbling, the man looked the hat over.

"These are quality goods," he said, his voice gruff and heavily accented. "Not the kind of hat I would expect to find a few streets away. The mark inside the band tells me this is the work of Mr. Keyes. He has a shop on Red Lion Street, near Holborn—very expensive. It is a fine gentleman who had this hat."

"Do you think Mr. Keyes might know who bought it?" Jennie asked.

"I know my own work and my customers," Mr. Geismar replied. "A craftsman like Mr. Keyes should know this also." He gave the hat to Jennie. "Tell your mother to come to me tomorrow morning. I have some work for you—blouses."

"Mother will be here," Jennie promised.

Mr. Geismar headed to the back of the shop. "Come, Jacob," he called over his shoulder. "You must help me write up the accounts."

"You can read and figure?" Dooley asked in amazement.

"Of course," Jacob replied. "I learned it at school. Didn't you?"

"Righto," Dooley said sarcastically, "while we ate off silver plates." He turned and walked out of the shop.

"Thanks again, Jacob, and please thank your father," Jennie said.

"Now what?" Dooley asked once they were back outside.

Jennie was excited. "Did you see how Mr. Geismar reacted?" she asked Wiggins. "He knows an expensive hat like this probably belongs to someone important."

"Then it's off to Red Lion Street," Dooley said, taking the hat from Jennie and tucking it into his belt.

"Is that far from here?" Jennie asked.

"A mile and more," Dooley replied.

Jennie hesitated. "My mother will be expecting me back soon," she said. "I don't know——"

She broke off at the look on Dooley's face.

"Across the street," he hissed. "That's one of the blokes from Repton Street. The ones who were kidnapping the long geezer!!"

Jennie tried to follow Dooley's frightened gaze, but all she saw was a broad back in a shabby coat. Then she caught sight of a face peering past the large, thick man—a thin face with popping eyes aimed straight at Dooley.

Chapter

DOOLEY GRABBED JENNIE'S HAND. "FOLLOW ME, AND do exactly what I do," he ordered.

Without looking back, he pulled her to the corner, then into a street full of two-wheeled hansom cabs, the four-wheeled carriages called growlers, double-decker buses, and lumbering dray wagons, all drawn by heavy draft horses. Jennie was sure they'd be run down. But Dooley darted into brief spaces in the flow of traffic, hauling her along.

A cab horse shied as they leaped under its nose, nearly sending the vehicle it was pulling into a wagon. Both drivers swore at them, one brandishing his whip. Dooley paid no attention, dashing round the rear of a bus to cut off another hansom cab.

Behind them, they heard more swearing as their pursuer tried to cross after them.

Somehow, they reached the far side of the street

without being run down. Jennie staggered to a halt, but Dooley kept pulling her along, rounding a corner and dashing through the webwork of back lanes. After the third crooked alley, Jennie had no idea how to get back to the familiar streets.

They cut around piles of filth, came out on a larger street, turned, and headed for a huge open-air marketplace. At last, Dooley slackened his pace as they maneuvered among the shoppers examining goods at the various barrows.

"We lost 'im," he announced.

Jennie took a long breath. But now that they had stopped their crazy race, anger replaced her relief.

"We could have lost a leg—or our lives!" she said.

"At least we got away." He held up the deerstalker cap. "And we still have the hat, even if Wiggins won't help us. I'll come up with something." Dooley tried to sound confident. "And you can help me. I can see you're ever so smart. Maybe we could go back to Mr. Holmes's place." His eyes pleaded for her help.

Jennie looked down. "We'll see," she said. "Right now I think we should be getting home. Our mothers will be wondering what became of us."

"I don't have a mother," Dooley replied. "It's just

me and Da, and many's the night Da works late at the docks." His tone was matter-of-fact, as if he were discussing the possibility of rain, but Jennie saw a brief shadow of loneliness pass over his pinched features. "But we don't want *your* mam worryin', do we? I know a shortcut that will get us home before you know it."

They were heading down a narrow alley when a man suddenly appeared ahead of them. He looked like a thug, unshaven with bloodshot eyes and a scar that began at the corner of his right eye and disappeared into the reddish whiskers that covered his cheek. Muscular shoulders in a greasy corduroy jacket seemed to brush the walls on either side of the alleyway.

Then a sharp laugh came from behind them.

"Now we got 'em, Alf!" A skinnier, shorter figure appeared behind them, blocking their retreat. Jennie recognized the face of their original pursuer. He was almost bobbing up and down with excitement, reminding her of a small dog yapping around the feet of a large, vicious mastiff. "I said if you nipped round this way, we could catch 'em between us, didn't I?"

The jittery little man pointed at Dooley. "I knew that head of red hair the moment I seen him again. That's the little bleeder who was peepin' in the window at Repton Street while we carried—" He suddenly broke off.

"Carried what, Twitter?" the thug called Alf growled.

"M-my guv'nor says we can't say." Twitter smiled nervously at Alf, then scowled at Dooley. "Had to go to a whole other place on account of you. Fetching and carrying over half of London." The smaller man glanced at Alf again. "You want to do for him here?"

Alf shook his head. "I think *my* boss would want to talk to 'em. So I'll take both of 'em along. You ain't goin' to argue, are you, Twitter?"

The nervous little man shook his head.

"Grand," Alf said.

"Get that deerstalker off them," Twitter spoke up. "Don't want that left behind again."

Alf glanced at Twitter, then shrugged. "Come along, you two."

He stepped toward them, reaching out a hand bigger than Jennie's head, a hand that could easily turn into a fist capable of pounding Twitter—or any of them—into jelly.

Whirling round, Dooley swung his shoe shine kit.

The wooden box caught Twitter on the shin. With a howl, the little thug hopped around, clutching at his injured leg.

Dooley darted around him, shouting, "Come on!"

Jennie didn't need a second invitation. She ran as fast as she could at Dooley's heels. Unfortunately, Alf was right behind her. He moved surprisingly quickly for a man his size.

Even as she ran, Jennie's brain made the cold calculations. *Each of Alf's steps is worth two of ours. He'll catch us before we reach the end of the alley.*

Dooley must have come to the same conclusion. Just ahead, a load of trash had been dumped against one of the alley walls. Moldering wooden crates and a half-broken barrel reached halfway up the stained brick barrier. Dooley tossed his shoe shine kit over the wall and began scrambling up the pile of debris.

He jumped to straddle the wall and leaned down, reaching toward Jennie.

She was already climbing, and judging from the terrified look Dooley shot over her shoulder, Alf was right behind her.

Dooley seized her wrists and heaved. Jennie flew up to swing over the top of the wall in a flutter of skirts. She was clinging to the top of the bricks, ready to drop down on the other side, when Alf lunged, grabbing for Dooley's ankle with a hamlike hand. "Got you!" he growled.

Jennie released her hold and caught onto Dooley's leg, trying to pull him over with her.

For a second, she feared the thug would haul both of them back. Then, with a splintering crash, the piled-up boxes disintegrated under Alf's weight. He lurched out of sight, and Dooley tumbled over to her side of the wall. They landed in a tangle of arms and legs but quickly sorted themselves out. Dooley took hold of the strap on his shoe shine box and led the way through the tiny back garden and into the tenement house that fronted it. They reached the street and began running again.

Jennie was gasping for breath, her lungs burning, when they finally stopped. There were no signs of pursuit. She leaned against another alley wall, not caring about the sooty brick. "We got away," she finally managed to get out.

Dooley, however, was feeling around his belt, a stricken look on his face. His hands came up empty. "We got away, but we lost the hat—the only proof we had that Sherlock Holmes is missing."

Wiggins clutched the broom in his hands, trying to sweep out the back room of the Raven Pub. Mr. Pilbeam, the owner, had agreed to pay him too much for the job. Wiggins knew the reason—Mr. P. was sweet on Wiggins's mother. Wiggins tried not to presume on Mr. Pilbeam's feelings unless there was a desperate need for money.

But now, with the Irregulars turned against him, Wiggins couldn't afford to be fussy about where he could pick up a few bob. Mr. Pilbeam's shillings were as good as anyone else's.

The pub owner was a retired Beefeater. He had served as a Yeoman Warder, protecting the Tower of London, and even kept one of the ravens who'd lived there as a pet. That was how the pub had gotten its name, and its mascot sat in a cage by the bar, amazing people by speaking colorful phrases it had picked up.

Seeing the awkward way Wiggins handled the broom, Mr. Pilbeam had quickly realized that his temporary sweeper had been in a fight. He had tried to talk with Wiggins, embarrassing them both. So he'd left, returning with some cloths soaking in a basin of cold water.

"Hold these against wherever it hurts," Pilbeam said gruffly. "It should help."

He left again. Wiggins opened his shirt, wrung out one of the rags, and put the cold compress against his bruised midsection. It did feel better.

He repeated the treatment until he could move freely again, then picked up the broom. There was only one way to return Mr. P.'s generosity and kindness. That was by doing a good job.

It took a while, especially since Wiggins had to take a couple of breaks with the cold compresses. But he had almost finished when Mr. Pilbeam came back. "Some friends of yours are looking for you," he said, stepping aside. Dooley and Jennie rushed through the doorway.

"Thanks, sir," Dooley announced, red-faced and sweating. "Wiggins, wait until you hear—"

Jennie put a restraining hand on Dooley's arm, remaining silent until Mr. Pilbeam left the room. Then they gave Wiggins a complete account of their visit to Mr. Geismar's shop and what happened afterward. Whenever Dooley got too excited, Jennie would cut in and keep the story going. As the tale came to an end, she said, "The two important things are that Mr. Geismar said the hat belonged to a real gentleman—someone important. And having those ruffians come after us shows that Dooley really did witness a crime. Otherwise, why would they care about being seen?"

Wiggins tried to hide the concern he felt. The hulking Alf that Dooley and Jennie described sounded like Alfie Sinnott, a bad character who often hired himself out as a thug-of-all-work. Wiggins had encouraged the Irregulars to pick targets. Sometimes it was useful to know the comings and goings of various villains. Tim Doolan had often kept an eye on Alf.

If Sinnott were involved, things were serious. Still, he forced himself to shrug and look bored. "We don't know this has anything to do with Tim, or Mr. Holmes, or —"

"They wanted the hat, didn't they?" Dooley protested.

"And the big one was going to take both of us to see his boss," Jennie said.

"That's right. The other one's guv'nor wouldn't let him say what they were carrying—or who," Dooley put in.

Wiggins picked up the broom. "And they mentioned something about Mr. Holmes, did they?" he asked shrewdly.

Dooley's eyes fell. "Um—not exactly."

Jennie shot Wiggins a sharp look. "But what about the cap?"

Wiggins opened the door and finished sweeping everything out into the alley in the back. "Who's to say it didn't belong to Alf or this Twitter fellow? Stolen, of course, or maybe bought secondhand rather than from this Mr. Keyes."

He frowned, looking up at the slowly setting sun. "The time is getting on. I bet our mothers are beginning to wonder what we've got up to."

Wiggins put his broom away. "If Mr. Holmes is involved, he can take care of himself," he said. "And he won't like us butting in. I followed him once after giving him some information. I thought he could probably use my help. Well, when he found out, he gave me a right tongue-lashing. " 'I'll request your aid when I need it,' he says to me." Wiggins grabbed his jacket from where he'd stashed it on a crate. "We just work for him, Dooley. We're not his friends or anything like that."

"But this time—"

Wiggins held up his hand. "If he wanted us there, he'd have left a message—*if* it was Mr. Holmes." Wiggins leaned forward to tap the shoe shine box Dooley had rested on the floor. "You've had quite a busy day today, young Doolan—but I bet you got very little business done."

Dooley's face went red again. "But someone could have been kidnapped—"

"All you have is a lot of 'could have' and 'maybe,'" Wiggins told him. "Maybe they're rug thieves. Maybe they're out to do in the Queen. Should we call in Mr. Pilbeam? He's just inside."

Dooley stared at him, his mouth open.

Wiggins tried to make his voice kinder. "I know what you're trying to do. But it doesn't pay—and now you know it can be dangerous. Let it go, Dooley. You know how people get by round here. We keep ourselves to ourselves."

Dooley didn't say a word as he picked up his box and left. But every stiff movement conveyed silent mutiny.

Wiggins was also silent as he led Jennie back to his house. But his thoughts rang loudly in his head.

Dooley isn't about to take my advice. He's going to keep pressing on to find Sherlock Holmes or Tim's killer. And if he does, he's going to end up like Tim . . . very, very dead.

Chapter 5

RETURNING TO HIS HOUSE, WIGGINS AND JENNIE found that their mothers' reunion had not been a joyous one. Wiggins realized that his mam was deeply embarrassed by their position. Seeing the lost and hopeless expression on the face of Jennie's mother only made things worse.

"We'll talk more tomorrow," Wiggins's mother promised Mrs. James. She put her arm around Jennie's mother's shoulders as she walked her out the door.

"We'll talk more tomorrow too," Jennie told Wiggins. "There's more going on here than you're saying, and I mean to know what."

Wiggins reached out and took one of her hands in his. Jennie almost pulled away when she suddenly felt a few bits of metal pressed against her palm.

"It's only a tuppence and a couple of pennies," Wiggins whispered. "But it's all I can do for now."

"We don't take charity." Jennie tried to push the coins back into his palm.

"And I don't give none," Wiggins shot back, releasing her hand. "Mr. Holmes always slipped us a little in advance for a job."

"I'm not an Irregular," Jennie reminded him.

Wiggins shrugged. "Me neither, not no more. But if you and Dooley are right, we're working for Mr. Holmes anyway."

"Then you *do* believe Dooley?" Jennie asked excitedly. "About Mr. Holmes?"

"I'm not saying that." Wiggins glanced toward their mothers, standing and talking just outside the door. "See you tomorrow. We'll talk then."

Jennie nodded, then joined her mother in the street.

"It's pitiful," his mother told him after Jennie and her mother had left. "She's a widow with a child, no money, no way to make any, and barely a place to live."

"Where are they staying?" Wiggins asked.

"A little hole-in-the-wall off Cambridge Road, near the lunatic asylum," his mother told him. Wiggins knew the area. The houses there had rooms that were barely larger than a cupboard, cold in the winter, ovens in the summer, and soot-covered all year round.

"Growing up, she was my best friend," his mother said. "I've got to think of some way to help her."

"It's not our business." The words escaped his lips before he could stifle them. "We barely have enough for ourselves."

Mam reached over and pinched his arm, hard.

"Owww!" Wiggins exclaimed. "What did you do that for?"

"If I've taught you nothing else, I've told you never to turn your back on a friend. Never!"

"I didn't mean that," Wiggins explained. "It's just that things are hard enough and . . . Oh, I don't know."

His mother placed a hand coarsened by years of hard work on his head, gently mussing his hair. "I know what you mean," she said. "Times are hard, but we know where to find work. We know folks we can depend on. Imagine what it must be like for them."

"I'm going out," Wiggins told his mother abruptly.

"Now?" she said. "You've not had your supper. Why?"

"To see if I can get wind of any jobs," he replied.

His mother eyed him appraisingly. "All right. But mind yourself—no fights." She smiled as his mouth dropped open. "I wasn't going to mention it with company coming. But I didn't miss the signs either. You hear me, son?"

"Yes, Mam." Wiggins dashed out onto the street.

It's all falling apart, he thought as he walked. Just a few weeks ago, everything was neat and tidy. He was making a little money running errands for folks. With Mr. Holmes and the Irregulars, it had become a bit easier. Oh, it took work to find lads with the right skills and organize them. He'd spent months doing just that.

He put up with Mr. Holmes's orders and quick temper because the man also was quick with their pay. But he wasn't one to heap praises on any of them.

If the "greatest detective in Britain" didn't have work for them, Wiggins never heard from him. Never had Holmes once made Wiggins feel like anything more than an employee—and not a very desirable employee at that.

Even so, Wiggins had been determined to do the

job right. And it had worked too . . . until that night in Upper Swandam Lane.

Once more, the memories welled up in his mind. Wiggins could see the theater district with its fancy folks and expensive coaches. The lights showed only dimly through the heavy yellow fog. Everything had looked a little less real that night.

Wiggins had been surprised when Tim spotted Alfie Sinnott among the coachmen outside the theater. The fog was so thick, Wiggins could barely see his hand in front of his face. But Alf was there, holding the door for some fancy people entering a very posh-looking coach. That had seemed odd to Wiggins. Alf was a thug and nothing else, so when he climbed into the driver's seat, Wiggins definitely wanted to find out what he was up to. That meant hitching a ride.

The fog ensured that no one could see Tim and Wiggins perched at the rear of the coach, clinging to leather straps. But they had to keep silent for most of the coach's slow progress for fear that someone might hear them. They'd argued upon reaching the destination. Tim wanted to continue on after Sinnott, his usual target, who drove the coach away.

Tim didn't want to descend the worn stone steps leading down to a doorway so thick with shadows, it resembled the mouth of an evil cave.

They'd gone in anyway, he and Tim—and after that, the fear, the darkness, and that horrible sound. . . .

Wiggins stopped and leaned against one of the streetlamps. This was the first time he had thought about Alf since that night. He'd put the thug out of mind completely.

But now, if Sinnott was involved in this thing, then so was his boss, Limehouse Lew. Limehouse was a weasely but well-connected local criminal. He specialized in setting up crimes, working out of the back room of a gambling club near Whitechapel Road.

If I knew what was going on, Wiggins told himself, *then maybe I could figure out how to keep Dooley safe.*

Wiggins had a way to spy on Lew's operation, but it was a dangerous thing to do, and he would need help. In the past, he would have called on one of the Irregulars, but now who could he . . . ?

An idea flashed into his head, a thought of someone he could ask. The trick would be getting him to say yes.

Chapter 6

WIGGINS STOPPED IN FRONT OF A RUN-DOWN BUILD-ing four short blocks from Limehouse Lew's headquarters. Even here there were decorations celebrating the Queen's Jubilee.

For such a small section of the city, the East End had one of the largest collections of nationalities in London. Turn any corner and you might run into a Hindu or Malay, Arabs, Greeks, Italians, Jews from several countries, or an Irishman. Poor folk coming to London from foreign lands, hoping for a better life, were likely to end up here.

The street he was on had a heavy population of people from the West Indies. Wiggins began asking where he could find Owens roundabouts.

A man sitting on a doorstep told Wiggins

the family could be found on the top floor. Wiggins entered and slowly mounted the stairs. Like many places in the East End, including Wiggins's own home, this house had known better days. The carved wooden posts holding up the banister were scarred, split, or gone. Everything was dark and dingy. No lamps or candles illuminated the way, and the glass-less windows had been boarded up. The one difference was the spicy smell to the cooking instead of the stink of cabbage.

At the top of the landing, Wiggins saw a door standing open. He could see a short, brown-skinned woman moving around in the room. She wore a long, baggy dress, covered by a white apron. Her feet were bare, and a mass of dark hair was tucked under her white linen cap.

Wiggins stepped in. "I'm looking for Owens."

The woman turned so quickly it startled him. At first she looked worried, but once she saw Wiggins was alone, her expression turned to an icy glare. "What you want him for?" she asked in a musical accent.

"I need to talk to him for a minute." Wiggins felt surprisingly uneasy under her stare. "That's all."

"We don't need no trouble round here." The woman took a step toward him, raising a steaming flatiron in her hand. "So, you be gone now!"

"Wait a tick," Wiggins protested. "I just want—"

Suddenly Owens stepped in from another room and placed his hand on the woman's arm. "He's all right, Mama," he said. "This is Wiggins, the boy I told you about."

"This is the one?" Owens's mother looked Wiggins up and down—the same look women gave wormy meat in the market. "No wonder he was getting a tanning. There's not much to him."

Owens strolled to the doorway. "What brings you here?"

"Wanted to talk to you," Wiggins said. "That's all."

"Really?" Owens's expression went from guarded to curious. "Can he come in, Mama?"

"I don't have time for no troublemakers," she replied, turning away from Wiggins. "I've work to do. If you want to talk to him, take him outside someplace."

Owens smiled as he noted the insulted expression on Wiggins's face. "Come along." He led the way up a rusty metal ladder and through a trapdoor in the hallway ceiling. Following, Wiggins found himself on the building's roof.

Crooked streets and decrepit houses spread as far as he could see in the darkening light. "Doesn't look any better from up here than it does down in the gutters, does it?"

"No," Owens replied. "But we live here, don't we? I mean, *both* of us live right here in the back slums."

Wiggins could hear the bite in the other boy's tone. "What are you going on about? And why would your mam call me a troublemaker? She don't know me."

Owens laughed. "She knows boys that look like you, and she knows what they've said and done to her."

"Is that why she gave me the cold eye?"

"That's some of it," Owens replied.

Wiggins stood in silence. Somewhere nearby, he heard meat sizzling. Unfamiliar spicy aromas filled the air.

"You know how it is," Wiggins said. "We stick to our own kind, try to make do with what little we have. That's just the way of it."

"Is that why you didn't get beaten to a bloody pulp today?" Owens asked. "Because someone stuck to his own?"

"You're enjoying this, ain't ya?" Wiggins growled.

Owens nodded, a small smile playing across his lips.

"Look. I used to have some friends around here, but we ain't friends no more."

"I saw." Owens rose, balancing himself on the parapet. Four flights down, no one seemed to notice. "Can't always depend on people just because they're like you."

Wiggins heard something in Owens's voice. "How come you aren't out with your friends from around here?"

"You should hear what some of the lads around here call me," Owens replied. "Your mate's skull ain't the first one I've scraped my knuckles on." He glanced at Wiggins, then back to the parapet. "You said you wanted to talk to me. So talk."

"Look, something's going on, and I need the help of someone I can . . ." Wiggins searched for the right word. "Trust."

Owens halted his balancing act. "Me?"

"You stuck up for me when you didn't even know

me," Wiggins said. "I call that a sign. Got to warn you, though. It could be dangerous."

Owens glanced from Wiggins to the street far below, then turned and sat down on the ledge. "Go on."

Wiggins explained all that had happened since they had separated earlier. When he finished, he saw a gleam in Owens's eyes.

"If you don't think anyone's been kidnapped, why go through all this?" Owens asked.

Wiggins hesitated. "Because I suspect that Dooley could be right, and I know he's not going to stop until he finds out who it is, or—"

"Or they catch him snooping."

"His brother got killed. I won't have Dooley getting the same!" Wiggins blurted.

Owens studied Wiggins for a few seconds before he got up, again shifting moods. "Let's be going, then," he said, businesslike.

"You'll help me sneak in to spy on Limehouse Lew?"

"It's got to be more fun than watching Mama ironing other folks' sheets," Owens replied. "How do we do it?"

Wiggins smiled. "Limehouse has his office on the second floor of a gambling hall. It backs onto an abandoned warehouse."

"I know the place. Looks like it only needs a strong wind to fall down."

"It's supposed to be boarded up, but the boards are loose on one broken window," Wiggins explained. "You've got to watch where you go because the floors are rotted through in places. But when we reach the second floor—"

"You've got a spy hole?"

Wiggins nodded.

"All right." Owens headed for the roof of the next building. "We can take the rooftops. That way, people won't see where we're going."

Wiggins ran after the boy. "You done this kind of thing before," he said with admiration. Owens just shrugged.

They soon arrived at the abandoned warehouse. "You give me a boost so I can catch hold of that board and get my foot set where the brick fell out," Wiggins said, pointing to a boarded-up window set high above them in the warehouse wall. "From there, I can get in."

"And what do I do?" Owens demanded. "Have a nice cup of tea?"

Wiggins gave him a grin. "You just wait—for a minute."

Muttering, Owens helped his companion climb up to the window. Wiggins pulled on the loose board, slipping under it and into the building. A moment later, the board pushed out again, and a knotted rope dropped out. "It's easier to get in once someone's inside," Wiggins explained as he leaned out.

He held the board open while Owens climbed up and inside. Then the two boys hauled in the rope ladder and let the board swing back into place.

As their eyes grew used to the dimness, the boys could make out stained walls, the plaster chipping off to reveal bare brick. Sagging wood floors led off to deeper darkness in the cavernous room beyond.

"Follow closely, and step where I step," Wiggins instructed. They set off into the blackness. Sometimes the boards beneath their feet creaked alarmingly. Skittering sounds in the dark showed that they weren't alone.

"I hate rats!" Owens muttered through clenched teeth.

Wiggins chuckled softly. "We have a cat woman in our building," he said. "She must have a dozen of 'em. Place smells something awful when it rains hard—but they keep the rat problem down."

"Wish we had a few cats with us now."

Wiggins led them to a rickety stairway. "Put your feet as close to the wall as possible," he warned. "Otherwise, you'll take a tumble." They came up to a smaller room and crossed to the wall on the far side.

The plaster was completely gone here, and so were some of the bricks. Cracks of light showed through the chinks. Wiggins knelt by one, directing Owens to another. They peered in to see a room done up as an office, lit with several oil lamps.

The cracked plaster walls hadn't seen a lick of paint in years. Two hard wooden chairs faced a battered desk with a stained and splitting leather chair. Limehouse sat behind the old desk, feet up, leaning back in his decrepit throne.

Wiggins hadn't seen Limehouse in over a year — Nat Blount had the job of keeping an eye on him. But the would-be criminal genius hadn't changed. He was a short man with a fat belly that strained the waistcoat of the crumpled suit he wore. A gold watch chain stretched across the expanse. As Wiggins peered through his crack in the wall, he saw Limehouse fish out a large gold watch.

"Wonder who he stole that from," Wiggins whispered, and Owens grinned.

Limehouse frowned as he looked at the watch, replaced it, then sat up straight. A moment later, a knock came at the door. "Come," Limehouse barked.

Alf Sinnott shambled in, looking disgusted. "I'm findin' out nothing, guv. They got me out chasing kiddies now."

"What's that?" Limehouse scowled.

"Their man Twitter saw some brat peering in the window at the Repton Street place we set up for them. They got the wind up and moved whoever—or whatever—out of there."

"You still don't know what these people are up to?"

"Not a shine," Alf replied in disgust. "Twitter told me their guv'nor didn't want any of our lot up there."

"Mighty close-mouthed bloke, our client," Limehouse complained. "What about this kid?"

Alf nodded. "Twitter saw him near Mile End Road with a lass. We caught 'em in an alley, but he let 'em wriggle away when I almost had them. They left this behind, though." He tossed the deerstalker cap on the desk. "Twitter had a powerful interest in it."

Limehouse looked at it unenthusiastically. "Do I look like the rag-and-bone man?"

Still, he picked it up. "I have a meeting with the gent what hired us," he said. "Suppose I springs this on His Honor and see if I can surprise a bit more information out of him. I don't like muckin' about for someone who keeps us this much in the dark."

"I don't think that bloke is one to get very surprised, guv," Alf warned.

"We can only see," Limehouse Lew replied. "Go have yourself a drink. I'll be leaving in a bit."

Alf Sinnott shut the door behind him. Limehouse took out his watch and put it beside the cap on the desk. He sat gazing at them, his pudgy lower lip going in and out, in and out as he thought.

On the other side of the wall, the boys watched in silence until Limehouse apparently came to some sort of decision. He abruptly stood up, tucking his watch in his waistcoat and stuffing the hat into a pocket in his coat.

Leaving the lamps burning, he stepped out of his office.

Wiggins pulled Owens back from the crack they'd been peering through, not speaking until they were some distance from their listening post. "Whatever is going on," he said in a low voice, "Limehouse is in it up to his fat neck. Let's follow him."

Chapter 7

THE TWO BOYS CREPT BACK THROUGH THE CAVERN-
ous darkness to the window with the loose board.
Wiggins went first, dangling from the window
ledge to find toeholds, then scrambling down to
the pavement. He left Owens to follow, darting
to the corner of the building and peeping round.
Now that it was fully dark, the gas lamps had been
lit and they needed to be careful.

Limehouse stood in the entrance of the gaming
hall, tugging the points of his waistcoat down over
his big belly. In the light of the hissing gas lamps,
the gold watch chain glinted against a collection of
food stains.

Stepping down to the pavement, Limehouse
set off. Wiggins beckoned for Owens to follow him.
Trailing this villain wouldn't be difficult. His wad-
dling pace could hardly be described as quick.

Limehouse made his way through thinning crowds around the pubs, cheap theaters, and dance halls. Soon he left the bright lights behind, entering a more respectable neighborhood. The dimmer streets had shuttered shops and fewer people.

Wiggins took Owens by the arm, slowing his pace. It wouldn't do to get too close and call attention to themselves. The boys crossed the street so Limehouse wouldn't feel himself being directly followed.

The street led into a small square, an island of deeper shadows ahead. At the far side rose a dark stone building—St. Ranulph's Church, Wiggins realized. Its steeple vanished into the darkness above the dancing lights from the few, scattered gas jets at street level. He gestured for Owens to stop as they came to the corner. In the open space of the square, they'd stand out immediately.

The boys crouched in a patch of shadow, following Limehouse with their eyes. He walked straight for the church—or rather, for the closed carriage parked in front of the church entrance. The man in the driver's seat kept his face in shadow and one hand in the pocket of his coat.

Limehouse stopped in his tracks. "I come with what Your Honor wanted, and a little more besides," he called, slowly holding up his hands. A large, old-fashioned key showed in one, while the other held the deerstalker hat.

A gloved hand emerged from the curtained coach window, waving Limehouse forward. "The key to the crypts?" Wiggins could just make out the voice inside the coach across the silent streets.

"Yessir. Dunno what you want to be doing down there with all the dead folk." Limehouse's voice grew shrewd. "Or who or what you might be leaving down there. Best take care, though, guv. In two days, this square will be crawling with bobbies because of the Queen's—"

He never got to finish his advice. The gloved hand shot through the curtain again, this time seizing the knot of his shabby tie. Limehouse gave a choking gurgle as he was hauled off his feet.

"Do not presume to speak to me merely because we do business." The unseen passenger's voice grew slightly louder but remained deadly cold. "Speaking about our dealings could be extremely unhealthy. On any day, millions of bits of junk float away on the Thames. Who would notice one more?"

The voice was posh, obviously used to giving commands.

The mysterious passenger suddenly released Limehouse, who nearly fell on his fat rear, stumbling as his feet hit the cobblestones. His hand went to his throat, and his voice came out hoarsely. "B-beggin' Your Honor's pardon."

Gloved fingers pointed to the cap that Limehouse had let fall. "My man reported your man's interest in that—and in the children who had it. Unwise of him—and unhealthy for you." The hand opened. "Give it here."

Whatever notion Limehouse had of using the hat had been frightened out of him. He silently turned over the cap.

The hand vanished inside the coach. "Keep your mind on the rewards you'll reap from this venture," said the hidden man. "Any other thoughts will result in . . . punishment."

A moment later, Wiggins heard the unmistakable sound of a cane rapping against the roof. Limehouse scuttled away as the driver whipped the team of horses into motion.

"We have to follow that coach," Wiggins whispered. "The bloke in there is the real one in charge."

Owens watched the vehicle's progress. "That

street takes them to the docks, but it curves." He darted across the open space. "I know a shortcut—a way a coach can't go. Maybe we can come out ahead of it."

Wiggins followed the other boy on a run down alleyways and sometimes through buildings. At one point, Owens pushed open a door and ran through a factory along a narrow lane between machinery. Angry shouts followed them, but Owens paid no heed. He continued cutting as straight a path as possible through the tangled back streets.

As he ran, Wiggins tried to make sense of what they'd overheard. Limehouse Lew hired out his brains and his gang to plan crimes—especially jewel robberies. "His Honor," the unseen passenger with the gloved hand, was obviously a client—a client who did not want Limehouse talking about their business.

The question was, what *was* their business? A major robbery? Where did the kidnapping fit in? If Sherlock Holmes had discovered what these villains were up to, Wiggins couldn't imagine them letting the detective live. But they were obviously keeping their prisoner alive. Could he have information necessary for the job? Where was the job supposed to happen? Who was the victim to be?

A breeze blew into Wiggins's face, bringing a brackish smell mixed along with the stink of rotting garbage. The Thames and the docks had to be nearby.

Owens stopped and pointed. "If we're lucky, our coach should come out that street," he panted.

Even as they turned, the clatter of hoofbeats echoed off the brick walls of the warehouses. However, the noise was coming from behind them.

Wiggins whipped round to see a grander coach than the one they hoped to catch, pulled by an impressive team of matched horses. Even in the semi-darkness it made a splendid sight—except that it was headed straight toward them.

Grabbing Owens's arm, Wiggins pulled the other boy back just in time to keep them from being run down. Tall wheels rattled past them. Wiggins had a brief glimpse of an elaborate coat of arms on the door and snapping flags.

"Egyptians!" Owens spat the word as if it were some kind of curse. His face became a cold, furious mask.

"What are you on about?" Wiggins demanded as Owens's eyes followed the coach. It rolled to a stop at the entrance to a pier. Servants with lamps hurried to light the way from a ship tied up at the side of the dock. The neat lines of the vessel revealed it to be an expensive yacht. A flag drooping from the ship's mainmast matched the smaller flags on the coach.

"Filthy wogs," Owens muttered.

They watched as an elegantly dressed figure proceeded up the pier to the carriage, accompanied by servants. The Egyptian noble stepped into the lantern light around the vehicle.

"They killed my dad," Owens said bitterly.

"What?" Wiggins turned round. "I thought he was a soldier."

"He was," Owens replied, "and they sent him to Egypt. Some local bugger called Urabi was taking the place over, so the government shipped out our soldiers to stop him. Mr. Shears saw it. My dad was trying to face down a mob with a corporal's guard—six soldiers. The wogs rushed them before the rest of the regiment could get there. Shears said it was like watching the sea wash over something."

His face was bleak as he finished his story. "They found my dad and the others under a pile of heathens. By the time all the fighting was finished, Egypt was part of the Empire. And my father got his own little bit of it—except he has to stay *under* it."

The passenger boarded, and the state carriage started moving—away from them, Wiggins was glad to note. He wasn't sure how Owens would react if they came close again.

Owens watched coldly as the large coach rumbled away along the dockside road, heading west to the wealthier parts of town. He looked down and kicked at a cobblestone. "It was eight years ago. I can barely remember what my dad looked like," he said softly. "Whenever I see that flag—and then, to see them going about in grand carriages—"

"Speaking of which," Wiggins interrupted, "what about the one we were following?"

Owens glanced up. "What?"

"Exactly. What about the coach that was supposed to come out *there*?" Wiggins pointed toward the end of roadway they'd raced so hard to reach. "We had some distractions, but I don't believe we'd have missed it coming out."

"I know the roads round here." Owens closed his eyes, his face screwing up as he tried to trace routes in his mind. "No, I don't think they could turn off before here."

His eyes popped open and he swore. "But they could have stopped along the way."

"That they could," Wiggins gloomily admitted. "We can spend the night searching every stable and warehouse from here to St. Ranulph's, or we can go home to bed."

Discouraged, he made his decision. "I have to be up bright and early—there's work for me at the Raven Pub. So we'll have to put this off."

"For now," Owens said.

Chapter 8

THE NEXT MORNING, WIGGINS STAGGERED THROUGH the front door of the Raven, heavy buckets full of water in each hand. A beer wagon had overturned on the corner the evening before, shattering a keg. Down-and-outers from all over the neighborhood had pounced on the chance of free beer, dipping their cupped hands in the broken barrel and even lapping up beer as it spilled across the cobblestones.

All that remained was a spicy-sour scent of beer in the air that made Wiggins's head swim. It didn't help that he had spent hours in bed arguing with himself before coming to an unwelcome conclusion. If it would stop Dooley from playing detective, he'd have to go to Baker Street. But what if Mr. Holmes was there?

Worry over what could happen in that case had kept him awake even later. And when sleep finally came, so did the all-too-familiar nightmare, the one where he ran in darkness with a snuffling, snorting creature coming ever closer behind him.

Just as it caught up with him, Wiggins had woken up, bleary-eyed and tired. At least now he had a problem he could get his hands on—the multitude of muddy footprints covering the pavement and the entrance to the pub.

London mud was partly dirt and mostly horse manure. "Great stupid beasts," Wiggins muttered as he splashed water from a bucket. "Why do they always have to do their business in front of Mr. Pilbeam's place?"

They didn't, of course. Horses left their calling cards all over the city. In the better-off parts of London, people made good livings sweeping the streets clear so the posh folk wouldn't soil their expensive boots.

The best they'd get in this neighborhood, however, was Wiggins and his buckets—at least in front of the Raven.

Wiggins had turned back to the pub to get a refill when a hand landed on his shoulder. He dropped the buckets, whirling around.

"Owens!" he said when he saw who belonged to the hand. "Don't do that!"

"Sorry," Owens apologized. "I spent all of last night wondering what you'd decided to do about what we heard."

"It's getting too deep for me." Wiggins sighed. "Limehouse Lew has a grubby finger in any number of filthy pies, but he gets most of his money as an arranger."

"Arranger? Of what? Flowers?"

"Crimes." Wiggins lowered his voice. "For a big robbery or burglary, Limehouse makes the plans and provides anything that's needed—tools, transportation, hideouts. . . ."

"Keys?" Owens suggested.

Wiggins nodded. "Whoever was in that carriage must have a big bit of business in mind. Is it big enough to kidnap—"

"You found out who kidnapped Sherlock Holmes?" a loud voice interrupted.

Wiggins whirled again to confront Dooley. Standing beside the boy was Jennie James.

"We went to your house this morning and learned you'd be working here," she said. "Did you find out something?"

Owens looked them up and down. "And who might these be?" he asked.

Jennie took his hand and shook it. "My name is Jennie James—and yours?"

Owens looked surprised for a moment, then quickly composed himself. "Just call me Owens."

"Owens helped me last night," Wiggins explained.

"I'm Dooley," Dooley piped up.

"So what did you two find?" Jennie asked.

Wiggins told the story of what he and Owens had seen and heard.

"So something is afoot," Jennie said.

"We just don't know what it is," Wiggins finished.

"We do know!" Dooley piped up. "They kidnapped Sher—"

"Will you shut your pie hole?" Wiggins cut him off. "If that's what happened, it's not smart to go around yelling about it—especially after those men tried to grab you in the alley. And what we heard last night seemed more about a robbery than a kidnapping."

"There is one person who might make some sense of this," Jennie said. "Sherlock Holmes."

"If he ain't kidnapped!" Dooley put in.

"We might get a few shillings for bringing it to his attention," Owens suggested.

"And if he's not there and no one knows where he is, that would tell us something too," Jennie added.

Wiggins felt his stomach clench. He knew he had to go to Baker Street. But if he was going to face Sherlock Holmes, he'd do it without an audience. "Tomorrow," Wiggins said. "I promised Mr. Pilbeam my whole day, and he's got ever so much for me to do."

"We can help!" Dooley said, grabbing a bucket.

Owens picked up the other. "We'll be done in no time." Wiggins could see visions of rewards dancing in Owens's eyes.

"It's pretty mucky work," Wiggins warned, gesturing toward the gutter.

Jennie shrugged. "Sooner started, sooner finished."

Sometime later, Mr. Pilbeam shook his head, looking around his pub. Outside, the sidewalk and gutter were spotless. The brass handles on the door sparkled, as did all the brass work inside. The whole day's worth of jobs he had given young Wiggins had been accomplished, and it wasn't even noon yet.

The pub owner ran a finger through the bushy mustache that curled up to his pepper-and-salt side-burns. "Finished it all—with the help of your friends?" he said.

Wiggins looked as if he couldn't quite believe it either. "Yes, sir," he said, baffled. "I didn't plan it this way. It's just—there's someplace we all have to go."

"We agreed on wages." Pilbeam reached into his pocket. He'd offered a generous amount, trying to help the boy and his handsome mother. Now, however . . . He took out some coins. "Even shares." Maybe that would teach the lad not to be so quick at dividing his labor.

The sweat-streaked faces below him brightened as they each received a shilling. Wiggins looked as if he'd bitten into a very sour pickle as he took his.

"Off with you now," Pilbeam said. "And thanks for your good work."

"A shilling apiece!" Owens was almost gloating as he walked along Mile End Road. "I can see why you like to work for that bloke!"

"Well, now the work is done—except for walking all the way to Baker Street," Wiggins said. "Are you sure you want to go a good three miles, maybe for nothing?"

"We don't have to walk," Dooley said, pointing to the entrance to the train station ahead. "We could ride."

"I rode a train coming to London," Jennie said. "But I've never been on one that ran underground."

"I've never been on a train," Dooley said.

"Nor I," Owens added.

"I've ridden them before, on errands for Mr. Holmes," Wiggins said. "The Underground is very different—and expensive."

"Well, we have money," Owens said. "Let's go!"

Chapter 9

TICKETS COST A SHILLING APIECE, EXPENSIVE INDEED. Heading down the grimy stairs to the platform, they quickly discovered how different the Underground world was. The air grew thicker. Coal-burning loco-motives pulled the trains, leaving a haze of sulfurous smoke hanging in tunnels and platforms. Wiggins always felt it in his eyes and in the back of his throat when he ventured onto the Underground. Before they even reached the bottom of the stairway, Jennie was coughing and wiping her eyes.

A uniformed man immediately moved to inter-cept them. "Where are your tickets?" he demanded. He seemed surprised when they offered them up, examining them carefully before he punched holes in them. Standing on the platform, the young East Enders realized how much they stood out. High ticket prices kept poorer people off the Underground. Businessmen in sober suits shot suspicious glances at them. Wiggins, Owens, Jennie, and Dooley stayed in a defensive cluster, making sure their tickets showed prominently.

Wisps of smoke curled among the yellow-glowing glass globes that contained the gas lamps illuminating the platform. Then a fresh supply of smoke billowed from the tunnel mouth as if a huge, fire-breathing beast were approaching. They saw the outlines of the train chuffing to a halt. Climbing into a compartment in the nearest carriage, they huddled together on a seat.

If anything, the air in the train carriage was worse. Most of the male passengers smoked pipes or cigars, and the coal-oil lamps providing light added pungent fumes. They sat in a smoky hush, transferred to another train, and rode on to the Baker Street Station.

Heading back to the surface seemed to release them from a spell of frightened silence. Dooley began chattering about their adventure while Jennie stood coughing. "A little longer in that contraption," she said, "and I think we'd have been smoked like hams!"

She stopped at the top of the stairway, peering into the distance. "Trees!" she said in delight. "You don't see many of them in the East End."

"That's Regent's Park," Wiggins said. "Mr. Holmes's place is over here."

Casting longing looks at the greenery, Jennie trailed after Wiggins and the other boys. The buildings along Baker Street were tidy four-story brick structures. Some of the buildings had shops in the ground floor, but most were residences.

Counting down buildings from the corner, Wiggins said, "This is the one." He walked up to the door, took hold of the brass knocker, and gave it a couple of sharp raps. The door opened to reveal a gray-haired woman wearing an apron. She gave the children a suspicious look—especially Dooley. "You again!" she said, then glared at the others. "What do you young ruffians want?"

Just then, a voice called out from upstairs. "Mrs. Hudson! Send him up."

Wiggins's heart gave a nervous thump. But that wasn't Mr. Holmes's voice.

Reluctantly, the landlady stood aside, and Wiggins stepped in. He heard Dooley, Owens, and Jennie scampering up the stairs behind him as Mrs. Hudson sputtered complaints.

He halted on the first landing to find Dr. Watson standing in the doorway of the flat he shared with Sherlock Holmes. The doctor was dressed formally in a long morning coat and striped trousers—just the thing for an important business meeting or lunch at a fancy club. Watson held a tall silk hat in his hands, and his usually good-natured face had a stern expression as he took in his young visitors.

"Wiggins!" he scolded. "How many times has Holmes told you to come up alone?" He held out his hand. "Now pass it along."

Wiggins blinked. "Sir?"

"Your message!" Watson's voice grew sharp. "Whatever Holmes sent you with. Come along, I haven't all day."

"W-we don't have a message," Wiggins stammered. He always considered Watson to be the human side of 221B Baker Street. Sometimes the doctor had even joked with him. Today, though, he matched Holmes at his harshest.

Watson shook his head impatiently. "If you came here looking for work, you chose a bad day." He stepped back into his flat and started to close the door.

Jennie pushed past the frozen Wiggins. "Please, Dr. Watson, we came because we're concerned about Mr. Holmes."

"I hadn't noticed you, young lady." Watson frowned but reopened the door. "Come in and explain yourself."

They entered a somewhat untidy parlor. Comfortable armchairs flanked the fireplace, and a note hung from the mantel, pinned in place by a jackknife. A dining table and a desk stood piled with papers and other items. The heavy curtains hung open, and sunshine glowed on the dull gold in the rich, wine-colored wall coverings. Jennie, Owens, and Dooley looked around with wide eyes.

"Blimey!" Dooley edged to one side, fascinated by the chemistry equipment set up in one corner. Wiggins quickly intercepted him. He remembered stretching out a curious hand to have Holmes snap, "Do you want to blow us all up?"

Jennie glanced around the room. "You expected a message from Mr. Holmes to explain why he's so late."

"I beg your pardon?" Watson said.

Jennie nodded toward the note pinned to the mantel. "That says Mr. Holmes planned to arrive back at St. Pancras Station three days ago for your meeting today."

"You can read?" Watson said in surprise.

"That's neither here nor there, sir," Jennie said. "What is important is that we may be able to explain Mr. Holmes's absence."

With Dooley's breathless help and a word or two from Wiggins, she explained what they had seen—and deduced.

"Kidnapped? Holmes?" Watson frowned in disbelief. "I'd like a look at this hat."

"It was taken from us," Jennie admitted. "But if you saw him leave—"

"I was tending to a patient," Watson replied.

"You might check to see what he wore," Owens suggested.

For a moment, worry fought with unwillingness on Watson's face. Then the clock on the mantel behind him began to chime the hour.

"I don't think it would be appropriate for me to go rooting about in Holmes's wardrobe," Dr. Watson said. "While I appreciate your concern—and your ingenuity—I'm sure there's nothing to fear. If any man in Britain can take care of himself, it's Sherlock Holmes. Now you'll have to excuse me, I'm afraid. With or without Holmes, I have an important engagement."

As he spoke, Watson shepherded them back to the door. Wiggins and the others found themselves standing out on the landing. Downstairs, a girl about Wiggins's age stood polishing the brass knocker. She wore an oversized apron, and bright red hair peeped from under a maid's cap. She grinned at them in a friendly manner.

"It must be interesting working for Mr. Holmes," Jennie said. "Does he often go away like this?"

"He's an odd one, and that's a fact," the girl replied. "We never know when he'll be home. Sometimes he turns up in disguise, like. You wouldn't even recognize him for the whiskers and such."

"Was Mr. Holmes in disguise when he left?" Owens asked.

The girl quickly glanced toward the back of the house and then ushered them outside. "Nah," she said. "He had a tweed suit and his deerstalker."

"Mary!" Mrs. Hudson's voice rang out from the back of the house. "What are you up to, girl?"

"Nothing, ma'am!" The girl winked at the group, then rushed into the house and closed the door.

In puzzled silence, Jennie, Wiggins, Owens, and Dooley crossed the street, then came to a stop. It had just dawned on them that they'd spent all their money on a one-way train ticket. Now they had to walk back to the East End.

"Could we go up to that park?" Jennie asked wistfully. "I'd love to see some trees and grass."

Across Baker Street, Dr. Watson came out the door of 221B. As if that were a cue, a carriage rolled down the street and stopped in front of the house.

Wiggins and Owens stared. They recognized that rig—the emblem on the door, the little flapping flags. It was the diplomatic coach they had seen the night before, the Egyptian coach that had set Owens off. The coach that had almost run them down.

And there was Dr. Watson, climbing eagerly aboard.

Chapter  10

Wiggins and the others silently watched the carriage rattle off. Owens gave it an icy glare. "Wouldn't bother with the likes of us," he muttered. "But off he goes with *them!*"

"Mr. Holmes always warned us about deciding things without having all the facts," Wiggins cautioned. "We don't know how they fit into this."

Owens kept cold eyes on the retreating carriage.

He wasn't the only angry member of the group. "So Mr. Holmes really is gone!" Dooley shouted. "Now we'll *never* find out who killed Tim. If you had gone to the man when it happened, maybe he could have done something."

"It wasn't as simple as that, Dooley." Wiggins tried to defend himself more from his own guilt than Dooley's words. *It* was *my fault.* The thought was a dull pain in Wiggins's chest. *Without me, Tim would still be alive.*

He could feel Jennie and even Owens turning to stare at him. But all Wiggins could do was look helplessly into Dooley's burning eyes.

Jennie put a hand on the small boy's shoulder. "It's a terrible thing, losing a brother like that." Her voice was soft. "But if Mr. Holmes is in trouble, we may still be able to help him. I think it's time we went to the police."

Three headshakes met this suggestion. Jennie's cheeks went pink beneath their sprinkle of freckles. "A person's life is at stake!"

"Doesn't matter," Owens replied. "The coppers won't take our word about anything. Only time they even look at us is when they have to nick someone for thieving."

Wiggins nodded. "We'd have a chance of convincing them if we could hand them the whole case tied up with a ribbon. Problem is, we don't know nothing!"

"We know someone was kidnapped—and Sherlock Holmes missed an important engagement today," Jennie pointed out.

"We can't prove it was Mr. Holmes who got kidnapped," Wiggins replied. "We can't prove anything at all."

"We need to find that posh fellow in the carriage," Owens said. "The one Limehouse Lew brought the cap to."

"Yeah." Wiggins frowned. "But he strikes me as a rough customer. He was pretty hard with Limehouse, and Limehouse didn't even squeak. That surprised me since he has a reputation of being a real devil."

"This Limehouse commits robberies?" Jennie asked.

"Usually he *plans* jobs," Wiggins explained, "helping to set them up and figuring where and how to break in places for jewelry or money."

"Lord knows there are plenty of rich folks in London," Owens said.

"The Queen's Jubilee has brought even more rich folk to London from all over the Empire," Jennie pointed out. "Not to mention foreign kings, Indian maharajahs—"

"And heathen princes from Egypt," Owens added sourly.

Wiggins shook his head. "If we just had a clue . . ."

The problem was, they didn't have a clue, and no one had a suggestion about getting one. Discouraged, they trudged back to the East End. It was late afternoon by the time they had made it onto familiar streets.

Dooley was the first to break off when a man asked him for a shoe shine. He didn't bother to say good-bye.

Jennie watched for a moment, then said, "My mother got the makings for a dozen blouses today." Excusing herself, she set off for the lodgings she shared with her mother and the sewing work that awaited her there.

"I bet now she wishes she hadn't tossed away that shilling on a train ride," Wiggins told Owens. He bit his lip, remembering that he could have had all four shillings for himself if the others hadn't turned up.

"Speaking of money," Owens said, "my mother has a cousin near here. He works for a newspaper, the *West Indian Advocate*. Keeps the presses going."

Wiggins glanced off toward Fleet Street, where many newspapers had their offices.

"I'll do a deal with you," Owens offered. "The *Advocate* is running a special issue, a guide to the Queen's Jubilee, and they're looking for newsboys to sell papers in the streets. If Mama's cousin can get us jobs, we'll go halves on whatever we make." He gave Wiggins a wry smile. "Your white face may sell more papers, but you wouldn't be selling them at all without my connection."

"Done," Wiggins replied. He needed a job, and he couldn't depend on Mr. Pilbeam's generosity forever.

Owens turned off down a side alley, and soon they reached the crowded pavement of Fleet Street. The crowd got thicker as they neared their destination. A lot of boys stood outside the offices of the *West Indian Advocate*.

One lad came out with a big bundle of newspapers and immediately began hawking his wares. "Read all about our Queen's Jubilee," he yelled. "See the list of foreign dig—" He paused, trying to remember his lines. "Diggin—"

"Dignitaries!" an annoyed voice shouted from inside.

"Foreign princes and such!" the newsboy improvised. "Includes a map of the grand parade!"

"We have competition," Wiggins worried.

"We won't have to wait at the tail of this line,"

Owens assured him. "I can get in through the back door."

Wiggins caught hold of Owens's arm as he stepped away. "Get that list of foreign folk here for the Jubilee."

Owens nodded, then hesitated. "Can you read it?"

Wiggins shook his head.

"Me neither," Owens admitted. "Good thing Jennie can."

Watching Owens cut round the building, Wiggins felt a spurt of annoyance at Jennie James and her high-toned ways. But he had to admit, Jennie had gotten them in when Dr. Watson was about to dismiss him. She'd been able to read the note Sherlock Holmes had left for his friend.

Don't think she'd do too well selling papers on street corners, though. He was chuckling to himself at the image of Jennie hawking papers when a shoulder rammed into him.

Wiggins stumbled back to find Nat Blount's ratlike face smirking at him. "How the mighty have fallen," Blount sneered. "It's better than beating you, watching you beg for work while the lads and I live soft and easy."

Wiggins sneered right back. "When the coppers

finally pinch you, they'll put you someplace a lot harder."

"You just need friends in the right places, that's all," Nat said. "For instance, Limehouse Lew paid plenty for my opinion. He's got a job going, if you know what I mean, and the only way in is through a narrow window. So he's lookin' for a little fella—someone who'd fit."

Blount put a hand in his pocket, jingling some coins. "He crossed my palm with silver, and I came up with the perfect kid—Tim Doolan's brother, Dooley."

Chapter  11

WIGGINS GAPED AT NAT BLOUNT. "DOOLEY? WHAT do you mean?"

"Just a little business." Blount's snaggleteeth showed in a nasty smile. "He gave me half a crown, I gave him Dooley's address—"

Wiggins didn't even think about it—it just happened. His knee flew up, catching Blount between the legs. Blount folded at the middle as if he had a hinge there. Wiggins's fists lashed out repeatedly as he screamed at Blount, punctuating each word with a thudding blow. "You stupid, greedy pig!"

Blount dropped to the pavement like a felled tree. The crowd showed only a brief interest in what had happened. The moment they realized the fight was over, they turned away.

Wiggins was standing over Blount, panting, when someone ran up next to him. He whirled, fists ready.

Whatever expression he had on his face, it made Owens take a step back.

"What's all this?" Owens asked.

Wiggins quickly explained what had happened. "There's no way we can go off selling papers now. We have to get to Dooley's house—right away!"

"What about him?" Owens pointed to Blount with the newspaper in his hand. "Won't he go tell—"

"Can't worry about that now." Wiggins set off at a run as Blount slowly began to stir. "Nothing's going to happen to another of my friends!"

The boys raced through the winding streets of the East End. Sometimes they pushed their way through crowds or dashed between horse-drawn wagons and carts. They scrambled across rooftops, opened the back door of a rooming house, and ran through to the front. The one thing they didn't do was talk. They saved their breath for running.

Yet words kept going through Wiggins's brain as they pounded along. *Don't let those thugs find him! Let us be in time!* Wiggins didn't know if they were prayers or threats. They just spilled out with every step he took. Tim Doolan's death had been awful enough. How much worse would it be if something terrible happened to Dooley—especially if it happened because Dooley insisted on pursuing Tim's case while Wiggins held back in fear?

Dooley sat in the room he shared with his father with only the shadows from the flickering oil lamp for company. He dipped his spoon into the bowl of warm stew Miss McManus, a neighbor, had prepared for him.

"Your father has extra work on the docks tonight," she'd told Dooley when he came home. "He'll be late. But he asked me to make certain you were fed proper."

Normally, Dooley liked stew, especially when it had bits of curried mutton. The problem was that Miss McManus was possibly the worst cook in London. Her stew was too salty, the mutton was stringy, and the bread she'd baked had been badly burnt on the bottom.

None of these bothered Dooley as much as being lonely. He missed his mother. She had gotten sick last winter and never made it to the spring. Dooley knew his father tried his best to make things work out. At

least when Tim was alive, they could do things together, and Dooley had someone to talk to.

Times like this, sitting alone in an empty house,
were the hardest. He rose and went to the window
that looked out on the street below.

In the dim glow of the streetlamp, Dooley spotted two men, one big and one small, staring up at his
window. The little man was Twitter, who'd trapped
him and Jennie in the alley yesterday! But the muscular man with him wasn't the same thug who'd almost grabbed them. This man had a misshapen jaw
and a broken nose.

With a sinking feeling, Dooley realized that he'd
seen the broken-nosed man before. He was the one
he'd overheard on Repton Street.

Dooley ducked back out of sight. "How did they
find me?" he gasped.

He took another peek out the window. Twitter
and his broken-nosed companion were crossing the
street, heading straight for his house.

Dooley didn't know which way to go. Should he
run down to Miss McManus's flat or try to hide in
his own home? A quick glance told him the second
idea was foolish. There was only a small steamer

trunk filled with his father's odds and ends. Other than that, there was nowhere to hide, even for someone his size. He was trapped.

Dooley heard heavy footsteps coming up the stairs.

They're coming to get me! Quickly, Dooley blew out the lamp flame, then looked around for something to use as a weapon. He was about to pick up a small stool when he heard another noise, this time coming from behind him.

Dooley whirled back toward the open window. He heard the sound again, a scraping noise, closer and louder. Someone was coming down from the roof to the window!

I'm surrounded! Dooley felt himself trembling.

He jumped as a shadowy figure swung in through the window and started toward him. He tried to scream for help, but nothing came out.

"Will you stop gawping at me and come on?" a voice whispered.

"W-Wiggins?" Dooley gasped. "What are—"

"No time!" Wiggins grabbed Dooley's arm and pulled him to the window. "Follow me."

"But I'm afraid—" Suddenly, Dooley heard

someone grunt outside his doorway. The door shook. Dooley threw a panic-stricken glance at the door latch as it started to rattle.

"Come on," Wiggins urged.

A loud thump sounded as the strangers threw their weight against the door. Wood cracked, and Dooley leaped for the windowsill.

Wiggins was already climbing up a long, dirty rope that hung from somewhere above.

"Why don't we climb down?" Dooley asked.

"Because they might have someone watching the street," Wiggins replied.

When they reached the roof, Dooley was surprised to find Owens holding on to the rope. He had even anchored it around a chimney pipe. Now he and Wiggins began hauling in their improvised ladder.

They finished the job just as the sound of wood splintering came up from Dooley's window.

"They're inside!" Wiggins cautioned. "Duck down."

The three boys listened as angry mutterings and sounds of furniture smashing filtered out of the open window.

"There ain't no ledge out here," came the raspy voice of one man.

The boys realized that one of the would-be kidnappers had stuck his head out of the window.

"No drainpipe for him to climb up neither," the voice continued. He paused for a moment, then demanded, "You sure you seen the brat?"

"I saw him clear as anything," Twitter's whinier voice insisted. "And I watched the building while I waited for you. He didn't come out."

After a brief pause, the hoarse voice growled, "Well, you'll have to report back to the guv'nor. I know he ain't going to like this one bit. Not one bleedin' bit."

The boys waited in silence while they listened to the men stomp out of the flat and down the stairs.

"That was too close." Dooley sighed heavily. "How'd you know they were coming for me?"

Wiggins quickly told him about meeting Nat Blount and what the boy had said.

"Natty Blount is running the Irregulars? But you're the leader. "

"Not anymore," Wiggins admitted.

"They turned you out because of Tim, didn't

they?" Dooley declared. "They figured that since you didn't care about him, you wouldn't care about—"

The look in Wiggins's eyes shut Dooley up. He'd expected anger. Instead, he saw a desperate wildness, as if Wiggins were fighting to keep from bursting into tears. "Tim was the best lad in the Irregulars!" Wiggins said. "He was the one who always backed me up."

"Then why didn't you do the same for him?" Dooley demanded. "Why weren't you with him?"

"I was. I only left him for a few seconds. Just a few."

Dooley leaned forward eagerly, but the words seemed to catch in Wiggins's throat.

"You can go on about this later, mates," Owens cut in. "Right now we've got things to do." He had been peeking over the ledge while Dooley and Wiggins were talking. Now he pointed at something down on the street. Wiggins and Dooley looked over the edge and saw the two thugs walking away from the building.

"They said they had to go see their boss," Owens said.

"The man in the coach!" Wiggins exclaimed.

"That's right." Owens began to smile.

Dooley grabbed Wiggins's arm. "What did you start to say a minute ago?"

"Not now." Wiggins shook off Dooley. "You said you wanted answers. Well, those two might have some. I'm going after them. Are you coming?"

"You don't have to ask twice," Dooley said.

"This way." Owens led them along the connecting roofs. They entered a building and were soon on the street only a block behind the two men.

The boys trailed them in silence for another three blocks until the two thugs reached a corner and split up.

"Now what?" Dooley asked.

"Dooley and I will take the one with the broken nose," Wiggins said.

"I've got the other one," Owens said. "Let's meet up back at the Raven later."

The boys nodded and then went their separate ways.

Dooley and Wiggins threaded their way along the busy nighttime streets, never losing sight of their quarry. Finally he led them to a warehouse on Gowers Walk.

The place had large double doors facing the street where wagons could enter. Set inside the right-hand door was a smaller entrance for pedestrians. Wiggins and Dooley watched as Broken Nose unlocked this entrance, letting the door swing closed behind him.

Wiggins dashed forward, grabbing the latch before it locked. He waited a few moments, then peeked inside. "It's safe enough," he whispered. "Once we're inside, stay close to me and don't say nothing."

Dooley nodded. The two boys slipped inside, walking carefully on the brick floor of a big, echoing room. A large wagon stood in front of them, and they crept along it. The sharp smell of manure filled the air, and Wiggins heard a horse nickering on the other side of the wagon.

He dropped to one knee, looking under the vehicle, and saw that someone had moved wooden crates to create a temporary stall, where a pair of bony nags munched on a bale of hay.

"Harry!" Broken Nose shouted. "Get your miserable carcass moving. I'm sick of wastin' my time."

Wiggins risked a look. Broken Nose had his back

to them. Grabbing Dooley's arm, Wiggins hustled the boy over behind some barrels as the thug continued to complain.

"Dunno why the guv'nor puts up with that Twitter. He's almost as bad as that local gang he hired. They don't deliver what they promise, and they ask too many questions besides."

Another man appeared from what was probably the warehouse office, adjusting the patch that covered his left eye. "I thought you said that Alf fella was all right."

"We'll see if he gets the other one. But that ain't our concern anymore. We got our orders. Time to move our guest again."

Dooley and Wiggins stared at each other as the men moved into the other room.

A moment later, the pair emerged carrying a long figure whose hands and feet were bound tight. Even with a wad of sticking plaster taped across his mouth, Wiggins recognized those sharp, hawklike features. Although the prisoner was bruised and looked tired and worn, his eyes were still keen, alert, filled with determination.

They'd found Sherlock Holmes!

"Move sharpish and get them horses hitched up," Broken Nose commanded the thug called Harry. "I'll be glad when this is all done with."

Kneeling behind the barrels, Wiggins watched the men easily carry Holmes toward the carriage. Broken Nose was large enough to make four of Wiggins and Dooley combined, and there was the other man to consider as well. Neither seemed to strain at all hauling their prisoner.

They'd found Sherlock Holmes, but what could they do to help him?

Chapter 12

WIGGINS FLINCHED AS THE TWO THUGS DUMPED THE detective onto the brick floor like a sack of potatoes. *That had to hurt,* he thought. But Holmes didn't even groan through the gag over his mouth. Wiggins wondered if the man was unconscious. Then he realized the detective's eyes were open—and they were looking right at him.

For the briefest moment, Holmes's eyes widened in recognition. Then he turned his head away. *He doesn't want to call attention to us,* Wiggins thought. *We may be his only hope.*

The broken-nosed thug had picked up a bottle from somewhere and took a swig. "Hoy, Harry!" he called to his one-eyed partner. "D'ye think you'll have those horses hitched before daybreak? We have places we've got to be. Mind you put your good eye on the job."

While Broken Nose was distracted, Holmes shifted, twisting to reveal his bound wrists. He had his right hand clenched in a fist. Now the detective opened it, and a crumpled wad of paper dropped to the floor.

"Here now!" Broken Nose glared back at Holmes. "No squirming, you." The thug backed up his words with a brutal kick in the ribs that nearly spun Holmes around.

Holmes lay still as Broken Nose stepped over him. The ruffian's heel came down right on the crumpled paper, and Broken Nose skidded on the brick floor.

Wiggins held his breath. If Broken Nose bent to see what he'd slipped on, not only would he find the message, he'd probably spot the boys.

Broken Nose, however, simply reeled on with a curse, more interested in keeping his bottle from spilling. Wiggins silently let out his breath.

Holmes's eyes went back to the boys. Wiggins made cutting motions with his fingers, but Holmes shook his head. Instead, the detective's eyes moved from the boys to the scrap of paper on the floor, now much the worse for wear. Wiggins nodded, showing that he understood.

Broken Nose returned with one-eyed Harry. "Your carriage awaits, guv."

The two crooks took Holmes by the shoulders and ankles, carried him to the rear of the wagon, and tossed him over the backboard. Climbing in, Broken Nose used a length of canvas to cover their captive and sat down beside him. Harry ran to open the door of the building, then clambered onto the driver's seat. He snapped the reins, and the horses jolted forward, moving at a slow, clopping trot. Passing the doorway, they turned left—toward the Thames.

They aren't going to throw Mr. Holmes in the river, are they? Wiggins tried to reassure himself. If they were going to do for him, wouldn't they have taken care of it here?

Dooley began moving forward. Wiggins roused himself, catching hold of the younger boy's arm. "No," he whispered fiercely. "I made Tim go out, and he got killed. Not you."

Dooley stared at him with wide eyes. "What?" he said. "What was that about Tim?"

"You heard me!" The dam broke inside Wiggins. "The night it happened, we were over round Covent Garden. Just as the plays were letting out, Tim spotted Alf Sinnott driving a growler. There were three men getting in. They looked posh—we could see their silk hats. But anything with Alf Sinnott in on it couldn't be respectable."

Wiggins took a deep breath. "Tim and I climbed up on the back of the carriage. We clung to it all the way from the West End to St. Paul's Cathedral. Tim got nervous, though, when we got onto Upper Swandam Lane."

"What's that?" Dooley asked.

"By the river, before you get to the Tower of London, there are places where people smoke opium," Wiggins said. "It's dangerous around there. We dropped off the coach when it began slowing, and I saw it stop in front of a house I knew to be an opium den. Alf drove off, and the three men went inside. I could barely see them in the fog, but something about the way they moved—" Wiggins shook his head. "You know how a bloke moves when he wants a drink? These lads weren't moving that way. They were businesslike. I made up my mind to see what they were up to, and . . . and I made Tim come along with me, even though he didn't want to go."

He shut his eyes, remembering. "Everything was pitch-black when we crept through the door. The air inside was warm and smelled funny—I guess that was the opium smoke. We felt our way forward—I figured we'd get to the back stairs and try to find where they might have gone."

"What happened to Tim?" Dooley asked in a hoarse voice.

"He was scared," Wiggins replied, "but he was a game lad. He wanted to get out of there, but he wouldn't let me go it alone."

"What happened?" Dooley insisted.

"I left him behind me and went ahead," Wiggins went on. "I figured at least we knew there was a way out behind us. So I set off, feeling my way down a narrow passage. Most of the space was taken up with a long row of—I suppose you'd call them bunk beds, set along one wall. That's where people lie down to smoke their opium. But there was nobody in them! All I could feel was splintery wood. Then I began wondering what those posh gents would want in an opium den where nobody was smoking opium. I was just turning round to tell Tim we were getting out when I saw the light."

He took a deep breath. "Someone had come up behind him, from the basement I guess, with a candle. Tim had nowhere to go. I saw his face. He looked frozen. I took a couple of steps toward him, and the light went out. Heavy footsteps came forward. I yelled for Tim to follow me and ran. There had to be a way out ahead of us, if only I could find it. Then I heard—this horrible noise. It sounded like some kind of animal was chasing us.

"I felt my way along the walls and finally found the back door. But it wouldn't open! I clawed at it until my fingers were bloody, calling all the while for Tim. A terrible crash came behind me just as the door fell open. Then all I heard was screaming—and that snuffling sound."

Although his eyelids were tightly shut, Wiggins could feel the sting of tears. "I—I ran. As soon as I got to the street, I went looking for a copper. When I found one, it was hard enough getting him to come along. When I brought him to the house, that was the end of it. He told me he wasn't about to do anything for a couple of street brats who'd gone into an opium den. I should count myself lucky that he didn't run me in."

After a long, shuddering breath, Wiggins went on. "I knew many of those places had trapdoors that could drop people into the Thames. So I went to the river men and told them to be on the lookout. That's how one of their boats found Tim. I'd hoped he would just be hurt, but he—"

Wiggins opened his eyes to a blurred view of Dooley. "I couldn't tell the others what happened or even Mr. Holmes. It was *my* fault Tim was dead. All I could do was make sure the same thing didn't happen to you. I could do that, and I have, haven't I, Dooley? I've kept you safe."

His eyes cleared to see the younger boy staring at him as if he were some kind of monster. "I said it was all your fault," Dooley shouted, "and I was right! You left my brother to die!"

"But I saved *you!*" Wiggins said in anguish.

In answer, Dooley spat in Wiggins's face and ran off.

Still crouched in his hiding place, Wiggins stared down at the brick floor and sobbed.

He might have stayed that way for hours, except that finally his eyes focused on the scrap of paper Sherlock Holmes had left. He drew in a deep breath and swiped a hand across his wet cheeks. Creeping forward, he picked up the note. It had been an envelope, and a coin fell through the tattered paper —Holmes had wrapped it around a half crown. Wiggins weighed the coin in his hand. A half crown was worth two shillings and sixpence—half a week's pay for a dockworker like Dooley's da. Jennie would have to sew a half-dozen shirts to make that much.

That much money would certainly get anyone's attention if they found it in the street, he thought. *I guess Mr. Holmes planned to drop it along the way somewhere.* If Wiggins had come across something like this, he'd deliver it to the address on the envelope, hoping there might be a further reward. Holmes was probably banking on just that.

He looked at the message itself. The envelope was nearly torn in two from friction between the coin, the brick floor, and Broken Nose's heavy boot. There was writing on both sides, but it meant nothing to him.

Sighing, he stuffed the note and the coin into his pocket. There was nothing more he could do here. He'd lost Sherlock Holmes, and he'd lost Dooley. Maybe Owens had better luck following his thug. They were supposed to meet at the Raven Pub.

Wiggins felt the paper crackle in his pocket as he started walking. Owens would probably get no further with that message than he had. It was just too bad that Jennie—

Wiggins froze, remembering what Broken Nose had said earlier about Alf. "We'll see if he gets the other one."

He hadn't really thought about it at the time. Finding Sherlock Holmes and confessing to Dooley had driven everything else out of Wiggins's head.

The other one.

The last time Alf had seen Dooley, he'd been with Jennie.

The other one.

When Wiggins started to move again, he was running. His mam had told him that Jennie and her mother had their lodgings off Cambridge Road. He dashed along the shadowy streets, trying to get there as quickly as possible.

His destination was still blocks away, but Wiggins could hear crowd noises. His heart lurched as he saw a flickering, unnatural brightness showing over the houses ahead.

He rounded the last corner and found a mob

gathered in the middle of the block, a sea of upraised, gaping faces illuminated by the flames dancing from the windows of the lodging house.

The crowd stood like spectators at some sporting event, but over their confused chattering rose an anguished voice. "My girl! My girl! Where is my precious girl?"

Jennie's mother struggled against a couple of men who restrained her from running into the burning building. Mrs. James coughed horribly, her voice coming out as a hoarse croak. "Someone please save my girl! She'll be burned alive!"

Chapter  13

WIGGINS DIDN'T STOP TO THINK. HE RACED INTO THE narrow building and up the first flight of stairs. There were only two rooms on each floor, and the doors to both were open. The smoke wasn't very heavy, and Wiggins could instantly see that the occupants had simply run for their lives.

As he started up to the next floor, the smoke stung his eyes and filled his nostrils with a foul, suffocating odor. Wiggins pulled his shirt up over his nose and mouth as tears began to run down his face.

The smoke appeared to be coming from the room on his left. The door was wide open, and through the smoke he could see deep red flames dancing as if they were living things—hungry living things.

"Jennie!" Wiggins cried out. "Jennie, are you there?"

No answer.

Wiggins stumbled toward the door. Fumes made him gag, and the heat was almost unbearable. He wanted to leave, to run back down the stairs and outside to safety—but he couldn't. Holding his breath, he plunged into the room.

Wiggins could barely see a thing. But he couldn't help noticing the flames creeping along the floor across the room and along one wall. For once he wished he wore shoes as the heat worked on the soles of his bare feet.

How can I find her? How?

Suddenly, an old memory flashed into his mind, a story one of his pa's friends, a former fire brigade captain, had told. "So I drops to the floor and crawls along like a baby until I finds 'em. Smoke always rises, y'see."

Wiggins dropped to his hands and knees. It was true! There were a few inches of clear air down here.

He took a quick breath, then looked around for Jennie. "Jennie," he called, his voice raspy and hoarse from the smoke. "Jennie!"

He saw her lying on the floor near an over-turned wooden table. Something was already burning fiercely on the other side of it, and the tabletop was starting to smolder.

When he reached her, Jennie lay still and life-less. Wiggins noticed a fresh bruise on her temple. *Did she hit her head when she fell? Is that why she didn't answer me? Or is she already—*

No, Wiggins told himself. He took hold of her arms and, staying low, dragged her toward the doorway.

When they reached the hall outside, Wiggins stood up, hoping to carry her to safety. But the smoke had grown thicker now. He coughed and gagged as he draped her arm over his shoulders and stumbled toward the stairway.

Jennie moaned and began to cough. "Come on, Jennie, wake up," Wiggins pleaded as they stumbled down the steps. "Wake up, *please!*"

Suddenly, Wiggins felt his foot slip, his body pitching forward into space. Jennie began sliding from his grasp. Blinded by smoke, he was certain they would tumble down the staircase and break their necks.

"I got you!" came a small voice out of the

gloom. Someone was struggling to hold them up.

"Dooley!" Wiggins exclaimed. "How—?" His question broke off as a fit of coughing racked him.

"Saw you go in, didn't I?" Dooley replied. "Reckoned you could use some help."

Moaning and coughing, Jennie revived just enough to stagger along with the aid of the boys.

Together they made it down the last flight of stairs, out of the building, and across the street. Some people in the crowd helped them sit down on the curb.

"Never thought I'd be calling *this* fresh air," Jennie gasped. She was still coughing from the fumes. Dooley and Wiggins sat on either side of her. "Thank you," she told Wiggins. "Thank you very much."

Wiggins wheezed a bit as he glanced up at the flames shooting out of the top-floor flat. "What happened? Did you knock something over?"

"No!" Jennie sat bolt upright. Though her eyes were still tearing and soot covered her face, the girl's expression of anger startled both boys. "I was attacked."

"What?" Dooley gasped.

"My mother went to deliver some sewing. I was sitting in our room, waiting for her to get back," Jennie explained. "Two men broke in the door. I thought they were thieves until they tried to take me away!"

"That's just what happened to me," Dooley replied. "They would have nabbed me too—if Wiggins and Owens hadn't got me out in time." He looked up at Wiggins. "I'm sorry about what I said."

Wiggins reached over and lightly punched Dooley on the arm. "Don't worry about it. But how—"

"Jennie! Jennie, dear!"

The three friends looked up to see Clara James pushing through the crowd of onlookers. Trailing after her were a few people Wiggins guessed were tenants of the building.

"You're alive!" her mother cried as she knelt to hug her daughter. "Are you hurt badly?"

"No, Mother," Jennie replied. "I'm just a little—"

"What did you do?" one of the tenants shouted at her. "Was you playing with matches, or did you upset the lamp?"

Jennie's eyes flashed as she stood. "I was attacked by two men!" she declared. "The oil lamp went over while we struggled. Then the fire started."

"What would they want with you?" another tenant demanded. "None of us living in this place got any money!"

"I don't know," Jennie said. "They knocked me senseless and left me to the flames."

"My poor darling," Mrs. James said, embracing her daughter. But the angry tenants kept shouting at them.

"Where are we supposed to live?"

"I didn't see no men!"

"My daughter does not lie!" Eyes flashing, Clara James faced the angry crowd, stepping between them and Jennie. For a moment Wiggins could see a shadow of the young woman she must have been. Wiggins and Dooley each took hold of Jennie's arms and slowly pulled her away. In the distance, they could hear the harsh clanging of a fire engine bell.

"We'd better go," Wiggins told Jennie.

"I'm not afraid of these people," she protested.

"I know that," Wiggins replied. "But we need you. And with what these folks are saying, when the coppers get here, they may take you in."

Jennie looked ready to argue, then sagged. "My mother isn't well. How can I leave her?"

"Dooley," Wiggins instructed, "after we're away, take Mrs. James over to my house. Mam will be up baking—she'll take care of her. Tell them we took Jennie where she'll be safe from the crowd, and then meet us at the Raven. Got it?"

Dooley nodded eagerly. He stepped forward to stand by Jennie's mother as Wiggins and Jennie melted into the crowd. Moments later, they were rushing through a series of back alleys on their way to the pub.

When they snuck in the back door, Owens was waiting there, comfortably stretched out in the back room. "What took you so—" He stopped, taking in their smoke-grimed faces and clothes.

Quickly, Wiggins and Jennie explained the events of the past half hour. Dooley arrived to add his own bit.

Then it was Owens's turn. "I followed my man down to the same part of the docks where we were nearly run over last night." He gave Wiggins a significant look. "You remember—where that Egyptian ship is anchored."

"Did he go aboard?" Wiggins asked.

"No," Owens admitted. "He met some blokes on

the pier, and they started some ugly talk about killing someone."

"What did they say?" Jennie asked.

"Something about 'doing in the old crow in her everlasting black.'" Owens shrugged. "I couldn't get too close. At one point, I thought they saw me, so I took off."

Wiggins punched the table in frustration. "Sherlock Holmes has been kidnapped—we know that for certain now. Limehouse Lew is involved, probably setting up some big robbery. There are thugs after us who won't stop at burning someone's house down, and the old Irregulars are working for the bad'uns!"

"We're a bit outnumbered," Owens said with grim humor.

"I wish Tim were here." Dooley sighed. "He'd be on our side."

"That he would." Wiggins glanced at Dooley, remembering their angry parting—and his timely return. "Though you did pretty well by yourself. How'd you find me at Jennie's after you ran off?"

"I wanted someone to talk to," Dooley admitted. "So I went to see Jennie, found the place on fire, and saw you run in the front door." He gave Wiggins a sidelong glance. "I'm still kind of mad at you. But I used to get mad at Tim sometimes too."

"I'm glad you came and helped." Jennie hugged Dooley, then turned to the others. "What do we do now?"

"We've found out how dangerous it is, trying to go it alone," Wiggins said. "If we're going to survive even this night, we'll have to fight back—together. I say we form an alliance, like. For protection."

"A league," Jennie added, her face lighting up.

"Sure—the Raven League," Owens said with a laugh. "We can hold meetings here in the back room of the pub."

"Laugh if you will," Wiggins shot back. "But if we don't hold together, those thugs will get us, one by one."

Jennie nodded. "I agree."

"The Raven League. I like it," Dooley said. "Sounds like a secret society."

"This isn't playing about, Dooley," Jennie said severely. "We need to find a way out of this fix."

"Starting with finding out who they plan to rob," Owens said.

"Not just rob," Dooley put in. "From what you heard, whoever it is, they plan to kill 'em too." His eyes grew sad. "So much killin'. I dunno why they didn't kill Mr. Holmes—except their guv'nor said he had a use for him."

"I don't know what use a criminal could find for a man who would put him in prison," Jennie wondered.

"We need to find and rescue Mr. Holmes," Wiggins said. "Let *him* figure out the rest." He hesitated. "But we need someplace to think and work things out."

"Can't we stay here?" Jennie asked.

"Those blokes will know who we all are now," Wiggins warned. "Especially after the Irregulars get talking."

Owens nodded. "It won't take them long to start searching out all of Wiggins's digs." A slow smile spread over the boy's face. "I've got an idea," he said. "Since Limehouse Lew is part of the reason we're in this, why not hide out right under his nose?"

"The old warehouse next door to his place!" Wiggins laughed.

"Where?" Jennie asked.

"I'll explain on the way." Wiggins went to the pub's back door. "Maybe we'll even pick up some information."

A little while later, Wiggins and the others had made their way into the derelict warehouse, settling near the cracks in the far wall. By taking turns, they could peek into Limehouse's office. The club was closed by now, but Limehouse Lew still sat at his desk, nervously fingering his watch chain. Then he got up and left the room.

Wiggins moved away from the vantage point and felt a tug on his shirtsleeve. It was Dooley. "It took me by surprise when I heard—when you told me about Tim," he said in a quiet voice. "I felt . . . well, I guess I showed you how I felt, and now I'm sorry. You done your best for me and tryin' to protect us all."

Wiggins snorted. "Fine job I did. We're hiding in the dark with a bunch of yobs outside who'd just as soon cut our throats as look at us. I'm not as good at this as I thought," he confessed.

"That's not what Tim thought," Dooley said. "Always looked up to you, he did. He told me you always treated him fair and square. He got even shares on any money, and that helped out at home. Tim was proud to be an Irregular. With him gone now and Da working all hours to get a bit more money, well . . ." Dooley's voice grew shy. "I'm glad you're around when I'm on the streets."

"Dooley, I—" Wiggins shook his head. The thing was, all of them—Dooley, Jennie, Owens, even Wiggins himself—were painfully short of family. And they were all in danger.

"I don't know what happened with the Irregulars," Dooley said, "but they were good because of you. Now you're with us, and we'll be just as good. Maybe better."

Owens interrupted from where he was peering through the wall. "He's back!" he hissed. "And he's got something."

Wiggins returned to the wall to see Limehouse clearing space on the cluttered desktop for a large, boxy package. It was wrapped in burlap and tied with a thin cord.

Before Owens could say any more, Wiggins signaled for quiet. From his vantage point, he could see another person entering the room—a gentleman, judging by his clothing, but Wiggins couldn't see his face.

He could see Lew's face, though—the criminal looked nervous as he sat behind his desk.

"I'm surprised to see you, Your Honor," Lew said. "Thought you'd send one of your lads round."

"This package is important enough." The visitor's voice was as posh as his clothing. It was the same voice Wiggins had heard coming from the coach the night before. "It isn't every day one carries an infernal device around London."

"It ain't so infernal," Lew replied. "Just a dynamite bomb." His voice took on a nervous tone. "You know I minds me own business, I does, but I feels it would do me good to know what ye want with one of them things."

The visitor remained silent.

"I mean, you pay well, but—" Limehouse's voice shifted to a whine. "I can't have none of this traced back to me."

"You are quite right," the visitor said as he reached across the desk for the deadly package. All Wiggins could see was his back and the turned-up collar of his expensive coat. "That would be inconvenient. I can promise you that however this turns out, it will be no problem for you."

The stranger's other hand went into his coat pocket and came out holding a revolver. When he fired, the shot seemed loud enough to bring down the damaged wall of the office and the warehouse beside.

Chapter 14

THE EAVESDROPPERS ALL LEAPED BACK AT THE GUN-shot. Pushing down his shock, Wiggins leaned forward, determined to identify the stranger. Through the crack, he could see the gross form of Limehouse Lew sprawled across the desk. But Wiggins couldn't find an angle where he could catch sight of the gunman. All he saw was a black-clad arm and gloved hand carrying the package through the door, followed by the sound of footsteps quickly receding.

The others began to crowd around the vantage point, asking confused questions.

"What—?" Jennie began.

"Who—?" said Owens.

Wiggins hissed them both to silence as the door in the room beyond rattled open.

"Guv?" Alf Sinnott's voice came from the entrance. "What was that noise?"

Then he obviously saw Limehouse Lew's lifeless form because he began to swear. The door to the club banged open, and Sinnott roared out into the street, "Get the troops—everybody you can find. The guv'nor's been shot, and whoever did it can't have got far."

Wiggins glanced at his companions. In the wan light coming through the crack, they looked scared. Now the members of Limehouse Lew's gang would be called in from looking for them and set to prowling the nearby streets, hunting for the killer. Wiggins had the uncomfortable realization that the Raven League might have moved from the frying pan right into the fire. The search would be hottest right outside their hiding place. And if anybody got the notion to take a look inside this warehouse . . .

To distract himself—and the others—from that thought, Wiggins said, "Looks like we may be stuck here. We'd best do as we said and try to work all of this out."

They moved away from the spy hole and settled in their dark surroundings. They looked at one another for a moment in silence.

"Well, I can't offer much," Owens said. "I tracked my bloke to the docks, heard him say that strange bit about killing the old crow, and then I lost him. End of story."

"The one Dooley and I followed went to a warehouse," Wiggins said. "He helped load Mr. Holmes in a wagon, then off they went." He frowned. "They were heading for the river when they left. Owens—could you have seen them?"

"One wagon passed when I turned up from the docks," Owens said slowly. "There was a fella in the back, but I didn't really notice him."

"How about the driver?" Wiggins asked. "Did he have an eye patch?"

Owens stared. "So he did!" He slammed a fist on the floor. "If I'd known, I could have seen where they went."

"At least we know Mr. Holmes is down by the docks," Wiggins said. "And we know who shot Limehouse Lew. I recognized that voice. It was the same man Limehouse met yesterday evening when Owens and I followed him."

"You're right," Owens said. "Limehouse called him 'Your Honor' then too, when he gave him the key."

"The key to St. Ranulph's Church—no, the key to the crypts underneath." Wiggins snapped his fingers, a sudden thought coming to him. "It's like that case Mr. Holmes solved. Dr. Watson called it 'The Red-Headed League.' The whole thing was a scheme to lure a shopkeeper away from his business so a crew of criminals could dig a tunnel from his basement to a nearby bank. They were going to rob it."

"The crypts are underground," Owens said. "Dead folks aren't likely to complain if someone starts digging a tunnel nearby."

"Leastwise, we hope they ain't," Dooley said nervously.

"What about the dynamite bomb?" Jennie asked. "And why would the man from the coach kill Limehouse?"

"He got his bomb—and he didn't need Limehouse anymore," Wiggins suggested. "Dead men tell no tales."

"Neither do dead young'uns," Owens said. "Or dead detectives. We need to find Mr. Holmes if we hope to get the coppers doing anything."

"We're getting off the path," Jennie said. "If there's a robbery being planned now, it probably connects to the Queen's Jubilee. Wiggins, didn't you say you and Owens had a list of all the important people who'd come to London for the celebrations? Does it say where they're staying?"

"You'd have to look and see," Wiggins suggested stiffly. But after a moment's thought, he said, "And that may be a good idea. Anyone staying near St. Ranulph's could be a possible target."

He rummaged around for the tin box of supplies he'd hidden in the room when he first discovered this listening post. Inside were a couple of candle stubs and some matches. "All the comforts of home," he joked, striking a match.

As the light blossomed, they all heard skittering sounds as surprised rats retreated.

"Wouldn't want *them* at home," Dooley said. "Da finds enough of them when he unloads ships."

"Or in barns where they haven't shifted the hay often enough," Jennie observed.

Wiggins set a little piece of candle atop the tin. "Is that enough to read by?" he asked.

"It will do." Jennie put out her hand, and Owens gave her his copy of the *West Indian Advocate*. The thin special edition was a bit crumpled from its time in his pocket.

"It's a long list," Jennie said doubtfully, glancing

at the candle. "The Maharajah of Jampur, staying at the Savoy Hotel. Mr. Simon Peters, industrialist of Canada, staying at the Langham Hotel. The Governor-General of Australia, staying with the Duke of Steyne." She cast a look at Owens. "Murad Pasha, representing the Khedive of Egypt, is staying on his yacht."

Owens scowled.

"This list will last longer than that candle," Jennie told Wiggins. "Are any of those places near the church?"

"I keep forgetting you're new to London," Wiggins said. "See if there are any houses round about St. Ranulph's Square." When that didn't turn up anything, he, Owens, and Dooley suggested other streets nearby. None of them matched any addresses in the newspaper article.

The candle was getting very low when Jennie said in desperation, "Maybe this is the wrong path after all. What about that note from Mr. Holmes? Did he say anything that could help us?"

"How would I know?" Wiggins drew the envelope from his pocket. "It's all tattered, we've been on the run, and—"

Jennie's gaze seemed to burrow right through Wiggins. "You can't read, can you?" she asked softly.

"No," he muttered, feeling his face go red. "I can't."

"Me neither," Dooley admitted.

"Nor me," Owens said.

"I've noticed that about a lot of people down here." Jennie looked around at the boys, then shrugged. "We'll have to fix that when we have time." She carefully spread the damaged paper on the floor.

"There's different handwriting on this side, and it's in ink," she said, squinting in the candlelight. "I think it's the address. Here's an *A*, *K*, *E*, and *R*, a space, and *S* and *T*. Part of Baker Street."

She turned over the paper. "This is in pencil, and the whole middle has been scraped away."

Jennie tried to lay the paper scraps flat, holding the candle over it. They all huddled forward in the dim light.

"This says 'Watson,'" Jennie said, tapping a crumpled part of the note.

"And underneath there—is that a two?" Wiggins asked, pointing. He smiled at Jennie's glance. "I do know my numbers."

Jennie tried to make out the scrawled letters in the flickering candlelight. "It might be a capital Q," she said. "It's next to a *u*. *Quite*, perhaps? Or maybe *queer*. I can't get any more of the word."

She kept looking. "I think this part says *peril*. This is *caf*—" She straightened out some wrinkles. "Or maybe *captive*. That's definitely *aboard*, but the next part is completely lost."

"What's the last line?" Dooley asked. "His name?"

"It's the clearest," Jennie said, frowning as she held the guttering candle flame over it. "But it makes the least sense. *O sir is . . .*"

She looked up. "Do you think he never got a chance to finish?"

"Dr. Watson is Mr. Holmes's best friend," Wiggins said. "I can't see Holmes saying, 'Oh, sir,' to him."

"Maybe it's some kind of password," Owens suggested.

"It's not *oh, sir*. It's just the letter *O* and *sir*." Jennie almost had her nose to the paper as she brought the candle close. "And the *sir* and the *is* seem to be written together. Maybe it's all one word, but I've never seen it before. Maybe if I sound it out . . ."

She made various tries. "Uh-sur-iss. Uh-seer-iss. Oh-sigh-riss . . ."

"Huh!" Dooley said in surprise. "There's a ship on the docks called that. My da helped unload her."

"A ship!" Owens said. "Didn't you say one of the words there was *aboard*?"

"Maybe we've got enough, even if this message got all torn up," Wiggins said. "*Captive aboard Oss—Oze—*"

"HMS *Osiris*," Dooley put in. "She's tied up at the East India Docks."

"That's a long way from St. Ranulph's," Wiggins said.

"But a good place to keep Mr. Holmes," Owens cut in. "The wagon I saw—it could have been headed for those docks." He grinned. "And if I had a crime in mind, the farther away I had Sherlock Holmes, the better."

"Right, then," Wiggins said. "We'll go down to the docks around HMS *Osiris*, nose around a bit, and—"

"Keep looking!" Alf Sinnott's voice boomed through the crack in the wall as he barged into the office next door.

The congratulatory mood in the warehouse vanished immediately. Wiggins swiftly blew out the candle, and he and the others crouched in silence.

The place was so quiet, they could hear the gurgle of a bottle and Sinnott's noisy swallows.

There's a hard egg, Wiggins thought. *Havin' himself a drink right beside a dead body.*

The door to the club opened to admit a group of men, from the sounds of their confused conversation.

"Pick 'im up and bring 'im home," Alf's voice cut across the murmurs. "We don't want the coppers getting too interested in what goes on round here."

From the grunts and mumbles, it was obvious that the yobs next door were working to shift the heavy remains of Limehouse Lew.

"And keep your eyes open along the way," Sinnott growled as the sounds of movement receded out into the club. "Whoever done this can't have got all that far."

"We know, Alf," a voice answered. "We fair been scourin' the streets roundabouts."

"When *I'm* satisfied, we'll move on," Alf Sinnott replied. "Shake a leg. I want all of you back out there looking for the shooter or anybody who may have seen him. Now, get."

One thing is sure, Wiggins thought. *We won't be heading off for the HMS* Osiris *or anywhere else right now.* They'd just have to wait until the searching thugs moved farther away from the gambling hall—and from them.

Jennie shifted. "Might as well make ourselves comfortable," she whispered.

The others followed her example, trying to find some sort of snug position in the dark dankness. The pitch-dark atmosphere seemed to press down on them, smothering any conversation.

Sometimes voices sounded from next door or filtered in from the streets outside. The trapped youngsters flinched each time that happened, but after a while, the dark, the late hour, and sheer exhaustion caught up with them. One by one, Dooley, Jennie, and then Owens fell asleep.

Wiggins was the last one sitting up, blinking in the darkness as he tried to listen to the thieves' calls outside. Were they finally moving away?

Give it a little more time, he told himself. *Then I'll wake these others and we'll be off to the docks.*

He struggled against a yawn and lost. *Just a little more,* Wiggins promised, even as his eyelids drooped. *Just a little . . .*

Chapter 15

THE THING WAS CHASING HIM DOWN A NARROW passageway. Wiggins couldn't see it in the blackness, but he could hear it coming after him, making that strange snorting noise, as if each breath were sucked through thick muck or slime. It was right behind him, Wiggins could hear its heavy crashing footsteps—

His eyes snapped open in darkness, and he heaved a deep sigh. It had been a dream, the same nightmare he'd had so often since Tim's death.

The crash came again, but now Wiggins recognized it as the sound of iron-shod wagon wheels against cobblestones. Sunshine was making its way between the cracks in the boarded window in the next room.

Wiggins ran to the window, peering through one of the chinks between the boards. Bright sunlight shone on the street below.

I can't believe I fell asleep—and for so long! He turned to the others. Jennie made little groaning sounds, as if the noise outside had disturbed her rest. Owens and Dooley slumbered on, the younger boy making little whistling sounds in his sleep.

Wiggins ruthlessly began shaking them. "We've got to get up," he whispered, wary that someone might be in the office next door. "Come on, it's morning!"

Jennie and Dooley were still bleary-eyed as they climbed down the rope ladder to the alley in the rear of the warehouse. Owens and Wiggins hauled the rope back up. Each in turn then squeezed under the loose boards and dropped to the pavement below.

Wiggins turned to Owens. "We need the quickest way to the docks."

"Let's see," Owens said. "We could start off taking Commercial Road."

Commercial Road was a big street, but when they reached it, they found an even greater crowd than usual.

"Right," Wiggins grumbled, "it's Jubilee Day."

Jennie looked around as their progress slowed to a crawl. "Seems as though a lot of folk got out of work today." She paused, reading a handbill plastered up on a wall. " 'In honor of the Queen's Jubilee, this shop is offering a special tea blend to all the London cabmen.' "

"Lucky cabmen," Wiggins growled. Was there no way out of this crush?

Dooley took hold of his arm. "This way, before we all get stepped on." He led them into an alley and through a maze of back ways. "This may be a longer walk," he puffed as they trotted down an alley that stank of fish. "But it will still be a shorter journey."

Judging by the sun, they figured it was late morning by the time they reached the docks. The area was quiet. Only a few dockworkers were unloading goods from ships. Many had obviously gone off to celebrate or watch the Queen's procession.

Dooley pointed. "There's the *Osiris*."

Wiggins followed his finger. The *Osiris* was a modern ship, with a tall smokestack rising from its middle and paddle wheels set on either side. Masts rose fore and aft of the smokestack, but the sails were furled as the boat lay moored lengthwise along the dock.

It looked like a humble workhorse compared to the sleek lines of the Egyptian pasha's yacht anchored across the way. Wiggins frowned. Was that nearness a coincidence, or was there some sort of connection between the two ships?

Owens beckoned them forward. "Let's get aboard. If we find Mr. Holmes—or even the bomb—we'll all be heroes."

"Not so fast," Wiggins replied. "Let's get the lay of the land—or the sea."

They got onto the wharf and took cover behind some crates of piled cargo. From there, Wiggins studied the *Osiris*. At first, he couldn't see anything moving. Then he spotted a pair of men lazing on the rear deck in the shadow cast by a makeshift awning created from a sail and some rope. "Looks like only two men guarding the boat," he said.

"What about the rest of the crew?" Jennie asked.

"Probably gone to watch the parade," Owens suggested. He turned toward the workers farther down the docks. "Except for them, it's pretty quiet round here."

"Owens and I will sneak aboard and see what we can see," Wiggins told the others. "Dooley, you and

Jennie try to find any friend of your father's working on the docks."

"Why?" Dooley protested. "I want to—"

"In case we run into any trouble, we'll need help," Wiggins explained. "Your dad's mates will believe you faster than the police will."

Dooley frowned but agreed. He and Jennie bent low, moving carefully and silently through the stacks of crates. Once they were far enough from the ship, they hurried down the docks.

As soon as their friends were safely on their way, Wiggins and Owens slipped from behind the crates and ran the twenty feet to the side of the *Osiris*. They ducked behind sacks of seeds and spices stacked near the ship's gangplank.

Owens glanced about, then signaled that all was clear near the gangplank. Quickly he and Wiggins hurried up, their bare feet noiseless on the wooden plank.

They slunk across the deck, approaching an open hatch that revealed a narrow wooden stairway going down into dimness.

Owens glanced nervously in the direction of the two guards. The men seemed oblivious to the boys' presence. "This must lead to the cabins below," Owens whispered.

"It also leads to the crew's quarters," Wiggins warned. "So let's be very careful."

Slowly and silently, they crept down to a poorly lit corridor. The air was damp and thick. It smelled heavily of salt, oil, spices, sweat, and rot. The boys tried not to breathe deeply.

There were only five doors along the hallway. Wiggins stopped and listened at each one. When he didn't hear a sound, he opened each door and peeked inside. But as they reached the end of the corridor, they still had not found any sign of Sherlock Holmes.

Owens looked discouraged. "Maybe we didn't figure out the clue correctly," he said. "Or they could have moved him before we got here or done for him."

"There's still the cargo hold below," Wiggins reminded him. "That would be a good place to hide someone."

The boys found another set of steep stairs that led to the echoing cargo hold and then lower still into the bilges.

There were no portholes this far down, and the oil lamps were not lit. Wiggins and Owens had to feel their way, keeping one hand on the wall and the other one out in front of them. The foul smell of filthy water trapped within the hull seemed thick enough to block their progress.

Suddenly, Wiggins's outstretched hand dislodged an unlit lantern hanging from the wall, sending it crashing to the deck.

"That's done it," Owens whispered.

"Don't move." Wiggins strained to hear if the noise had attracted any attention. Nothing. "Let's keep going," he whispered. "At least a little more."

A couple of paces onward, they found the way blocked. "Here's a door handle," Owens reported.

They gently opened the door. Although no light had leaked out from under the entryway, the space beyond was lit. An oil lamp burned in the far corner.

Machinery filled most of the room, some sort of pumps, perhaps to force water out of the hull. It blocked their view to the end of the room that was lit by the lamp. Wiggins and Owens carefully advanced to find a cot tucked in the small open space, with a bundle tossed on it. No, not a bundle, but a long, thin person.

Sherlock Holmes lay on his side, his hands and feet still securely tied, the adhesive plaster still over his mouth. His eyes were closed, and he wasn't moving.

Wiggins and Owens rushed to him.

"He's barely breathing," Owens said, placing his ear to the detective's face. "I'll untie him. You take this plaster off."

Wiggins had trouble removing the adhesive. Holmes hadn't shaved in days, so pulling at the plaster meant removing his growth of beard and even bits of flesh. The detective grimaced, his eyelids tightening, but he made no sounds of pain. Nor did his eyes open.

Once he'd freed the detective's mouth, Wiggins put an ear to Holmes's chest, listening for a heartbeat.

"Do you think he's dying?" Owens asked, undoing the ropes.

"Of course not," came a raspy voice.

Wiggins jumped back from the bed, almost tripping over Owens.

Sherlock Holmes opened his eyes and gingerly rubbed his wrists.

"You're alive!" Wiggins exclaimed.

"I should hope so," Holmes said. "But kindly do not celebrate that fact too loudly, Wiggins." He coughed a little, trying to clear his throat. "I was employing some yogi breathing techniques to refresh the body and the mind," he explained. "My quarters have been somewhat . . . restraining."

"Er—right." Wiggins wasn't sure what else to say. "We've come to get you out of here."

Holmes's penetrating eyes glanced up and down the two boys. "I know Wiggins here. But I don't know you, young man," he said to Owens. "Of British and West Indian origin, I'd say. My condolences for the loss of your father. No doubt he died bravely in Egypt."

Owens stood rigid with shock. Wiggins, who'd seen Holmes pull this apparent mind-reading trick many times before, did his best to hide a smile.

"How could you—"

Holmes slowly rose to sit up on the cot. "Your ethnic origins are obvious to the trained eye," he explained. "When you leaned over me, I noted the military decoration on the chain around your neck."

As if in a trance, Owens fished out the chain from under his shirt.

"Yes. The Egypt Medal, as I thought. If your father were alive, it would be on his uniform, not around your neck. The deduction was obvious."

Wiggins stared at Owens. "I never saw that," he said.

"You failed to *observe*, Wiggins," Holmes repri-manded. "How many times have I told you that? But none of this is of great importance at present. I take it you retrieved the message I dropped."

Wiggins nodded. "There wasn't all that much left of it after being stepped on by that bloke with the broken nose," he said. "We managed to figure out what it meant anyway."

"We're here to rescue you," Owens said.

"Just grand, that is, lads," a gruff voice said be-hind Owens. "But who's going to rescue *you*?"

The boys turned to see one of the crewmen standing in the doorway. Wiggins recognized him immediately—the big, broken-nosed ruffian who had taken Holmes from the warehouse. The hulk-ing man's right hand rested on the door frame near the hinges. His left hand held a pistol aimed squarely at Sherlock Holmes.

"The guv'nor told us we had to keep you alive—"

"Well, that is of some comfort," Holmes said.

"Until later today, when we slit your throat and leave you to be found on that wog boat across the way to throw suspicion onto them," the man fin-ished. "That is, unless someone found you first."

A smile twisted the man's damaged face. "Got nothing smart to say now?" He began to laugh so heartily, he had to fight for breath, sucking air through his damaged nose. The snuffling sound made Wiggins stare. He'd heard it before—pursuing him in bad dreams almost every night since Tim Doolan died.

"You!" Wiggins gasped. "You were there in Upper Swandam Lane! You're the one who killed Tim!"

Broken Nose's snuffling became louder as he rasped through several surprised, quick breaths.

"That sound!" Wiggins cried. "I thought it was some kind of monster!"

Broken Nose gave a phlegmy chuckle. "Only happens when I breathe deep," he said, "like when I'm running."

He gave Wiggins an almost-friendly look. "So you was the one that got away. The guv'nor had to meet some people, private, like. I was supposed to make sure nobody disturbed them. Shouldn't have been all that hard, in a deserted opium den. Instead, I found a pair of kids nosing around. Well, the guv'nor gave me the word, so I took care of that—halfway. Now I get to finish it."

Wiggins's anger rose inside him like a living thing. He wanted to tear into the man before him, but he also knew he had no chance against the man's muscles or his weapon—until Broken Nose hefted his pistol. Suddenly, Wiggins noticed where the man had placed his other hand, and a daring idea came to him.

"I hope puttin' a bullet in you won't ruin the guv'nor's plans," the man told Holmes as he aimed his pistol. "He's got enough goin' on today. And we can slit your throat too—"

"Get down!" Wiggins shouted as he leaped forward.

The sound of the gunshot echoed like a cannon blast in the confined room. The bullet whistled as it flew past Wiggins's ear to strike the wall above Holmes's head. Wiggins slammed into the door, crushing the thug's fingers in the doorjamb.

The thug's yowl was cut off when Holmes threw the metal kerosene lantern across the room. It struck the huge man on the forehead with a loud clang, knocking him to the floor.

Wiggins started to lunge at the fallen thug, but Owens pulled him out the door. "Not now!" he shouted. "He's only dizzy, and he still has the gun."

"He's right," Holmes said, staggering across the room. "That shot will bring others!"

Holmes followed the boys out the door, but the great detective was moving slowly.

"Hurry, Mr. Holmes!" Wiggins called back to him. "That bloke is coming round!"

Broken Nose staggered to his feet just as Holmes reached the doorway. He lunged at the detective, but Holmes grabbed his arm and quickly shifted to his right. Broken Nose seemed to fly through the air, landing on the floor of the pump room, where he didn't move.

"That was amazing!" Owens exclaimed.

"I have studied several forms of combat," Holmes explained as he closed the door. "I find it useful for times like these." He slammed the bolt in place. "Now I suggest we move with great haste."

As they climbed the stairs, Wiggins noticed that Holmes staggered a bit. "Are you hurt?" he asked.

"I'm afraid the circulation has not quite returned to my legs," Holmes replied. "The result of being tied up for so long."

The boys and Holmes burst out onto the deck.

"It looks clear," Wiggins called. "Let's go!"

"Wiggins!"

Owens's warning came too late. A crewman jumped out from behind the wheelhouse, a large knife in his hand.

"Going somewhere?" the man growled through clenched teeth.

Holmes moved in front of the boys. "They are children," he said. "Your fight is with me."

"They got mouths, don't they?" the crewman replied as he stepped forward. "After I slice yer throats, it won't—"

"What's all this?" a voice interrupted.

They all turned to see a group of burly dock-workers stepping from the gangplank.

"See? They're kidnappers!" Dooley shouted, pointing.

The sailor retreated, slashing the air with his knife. "Get off this ship! I'll gut the lot of you!"

"You see? They're *dangerous* kidnappers, Officer," Jennie added as she led a policeman aboard. "You may want to call for reinforcements."

The outnumbered sailor leaped to the top of a hatch, stomping his feet, as the policeman raised his whistle.

From the rear deck, a hatch cover burst open under the sailcloth awning, landing with a crash.

The noise almost drowned out the shrill tweeting from the constable's whistle.

"Mr. Holmes!" Wiggins shouted. "Look!"

Holmes turned so he had the rail of the ship behind him. "I'm afraid, my young friends, we're about to have some hostile company." The detective's gaunt face was grim. "And even with assistance at hand, I fear we may not rise to the challenge."

Chapter

THE SHIP'S CREW CAME SWARMING OUT OF THE OPENED hatch, brandishing knives and improvised clubs. Charging across the deck of the *Osiris*, the sailors attacked the dockers and even the police constable with Jennie.

"We're outnumbered!" Dooley shouted.

"Not necessarily," Owens replied. He pointed to a number of policemen arriving in response to the whistle, batons at the ready. The big sticks rose and fell, and the sailors retreated, becoming more and more desperate as they were hemmed in.

The members of the Raven League didn't stand idle as the fray swirled around them. Wiggins and Owens threw things to blind or distract the attackers until a dockworker or policeman could deal with them. Dooley snapped a length of rope, tripping one sailor. Jennie swung a discarded club sharply against the wrist of another, causing the thug to drop his weapon.

The broken-nosed thug who'd been guarding Sherlock Holmes came stumbling up from below, his revolver waving in his good hand. "I'll kill you little blighters!" he yelled.

The man halted in shock when he saw the police uniforms and crowd of furious dockworkers. He whipped around, searching for Holmes. When he spotted the tall form of the detective, the gunman aimed his weapon, a demonic look in his eyes.

Wiggins saw him and screamed, "He's got a gun! Stop him!" A struggling sailor and two policemen blocked his way. Holmes heard, but he was trapped against the ship's railing.

Then a wooden belaying pin from the ship's rigging soared through the air to catch the gunman in the face. He staggered back and his shot went wild, flying up into the sails above. Wiggins turned and saw Owens's grinning face. The boy stood balanced on the rail, one hand clinging to a line beside a hole where a belaying pin had stood.

Two coppers and a dockworker tackled the

gunman, bringing him down to the deck. "Take good care of that one," Holmes directed. "He confessed a murder to me."

At that point, the fight went out of the sailors. They began raising their hands, surrendering.

Wiggins took in a long, shuddering breath. They'd won! Not only had they saved Sherlock Holmes, but they had also caught Tim's killer! The desire to strike out at the killer was still strong, but Wiggins knew he should step back and let the great detective take charge. Mr. Holmes would direct the police to haul in Limehouse Lew's gang and put the handcuffs on the mysterious man in the coach, whatever he was up to.

When he glanced over at Holmes, however, the man did not look like a triumphant winner. He knelt over Broken Nose, who still lay unconscious. Holmes's eyes blazed with anxiety as he rose up, beckoning Wiggins over.

"This blackguard won't be talking for a while yet," Holmes said. "We'd best search the captain's cabin for any further evidence we can find about their plan. Bring your lads and—er—the young lady and follow me."

The captain's quarters turned out to be a cramped room with a bunk, a small table covered with charts and papers, and several chests containing clothes, navigational tools, and other items. Upon learning Jennie could read, Holmes installed her at the chart table, instructing her to read every piece of paper. The boys helped him search the rest of the cabin for whatever they might find that could shed light on the diabolical plot.

"I must thank you all for your help—both earlier and now," Holmes said, thumping the beams and ceiling in search of hollow hiding places. "If you had not turned up in that warehouse—"

"We were looking before that," Wiggins said. "Dooley brought us into it. He saw you being carried into that lodging house on Repton Street and tried to spy on them. He didn't find you, but the kidnappers had left your cap."

Holmes nodded as he continued rapping. "I'll miss that deerstalker," he muttered.

"A couple of bad characters got hold of it. When Dooley described one of them, I recognized Alf Sinnott," Wiggins explained.

"Sinnott." Holmes frowned in thought. "He's a

lieutenant of Lewis Webb, known more colorfully as 'Limehouse Lew.'"

Wiggins nodded. "We expect Limehouse was helping someone with a job, maybe a robbery."

"He gave this posh bloke a dynamite bomb," Dooley piped up from where he was poking around under the captain's bed. "I think they're going to blow up the Raven Pub."

"What?" Wiggins and the others stared at him.

Dooley crawled out from under the bed and sat on the floor. "Remember what Owens told us those sailors said?" he said. "How they were going to do in the old crow in her everlasting black? The Raven is the only place I know of with a black bird—"

"He might have meant the Tower of London, where they keep the Crown Jewels!" Jennie exclaimed from the table. "A flock of ravens lives there, and legend says that if they die, the Empire will fall."

"That makes more sense than the pub," Owens said.

"They'd have to go through a lot to get a bomb near there," Wiggins said. "Why do all that just to wipe out a bunch of birds?"

"Not a bird." Holmes stopped searching. "There

is a *woman* who has worn black ever since her husband died years ago," he said. "A very famous woman—"

"The Queen!" Jennie gasped.

Holmes gave her a tight nod. "It wouldn't be the first time. There have been numerous plots against Her Majesty's life over the years. What distinguishes this one, however, is this bomb—and the number of suspects. It seems as if every group with some grievance against the Empire has become more active of late." He went back to his search.

"Like the Egyptians?" Owens asked as he and Wiggins picked up the captain's mattress and peered under it.

"Indeed," Holmes replied. "Although an Egyptian gave us the first warning that something large and dangerous was afoot."

Owens appeared stunned by the news. "An *Egyptian* warned you?" He and Wiggins replaced the mattress.

"Murad Pasha has no great love for Britain," Holmes explained. "However, he also has no desire to see his countrymen die in an ill-considered revolt. When he became aware of strangers fanning the flames of resentment in his country, he contacted my brother, Mycroft, who in turn asked me to look into the matter."

The young members of the Raven League stopped their tasks to look at each other.

"So that was the appointment mentioned in the note on your mantelpiece," Jennie said. "And that's why Dr. Watson went off in the coach with the Egyptian flags!"

Holmes frowned. "The unrest in Egypt turned out to be only the tip of the proverbial iceberg."

"What do you mean, sir?" Jennie asked.

"The Egyptian revolutionaries were spending money where they had not had any previously," the detective explained. "So were the Irish nationalists, restless groups in India, and even certain organizations here in Britain."

"Here?" Wiggins asked.

"Even in Britain, you can find those who believe in overturning the established order—revolutionaries, anarchists," Holmes said.

"With all this going on, why did you leave London before your meeting?" Wiggins wondered.

"I went out to the country to see a man." Holmes gave a wry smile. "I suppose you might call him a

retired anarchist. Although he supported the movement at first, in his later years he came to repent the
actions of his youth. Poor Lemuel still had many
contacts in anarchist organizations, however."

"Why *poor* Lemuel?" Dooley asked.

"He was another one who sent me warning."
Sadness filled Holmes's gaunt face. "The anarchists
were suddenly receiving a great deal of money,
none of it from the usual sources. Lemuel became
suspicious, and I enlisted his aid in tracing whence
this money came. His early findings suggested that
the plot ran even deeper than I suspected."

The detective's lips twisted. "His willingness
to help turned out to be his doom—he must have
been discovered. I received a telegram, supposedly
from Lemuel, asking me to meet him at his place,
hinting of great results. When I arrived, I found
the man dead and an ambush awaiting me."

Holmes finished his tapping and now began
searching the chests for secret compartments. "I
expected to die, but it's a far more devilish game
these people play."

"You think the Irish, Egyptians, and all are
working together to kill the Queen?" Owens
asked.

Holmes shook his head. "The people being stirred to rebellion are simply being used. That's the most devilish part of this conspiracy."

He looked at his young audience. "All through the Queen's reign, before you or even I was born, there has been a slow progress toward greater freedom here in Britain. More and more common people have won the right to vote in elections. Success in business, the professions of law and medicine, and even the military has become less a question of noble ancestors and more a matter of effort and ability."

Wiggins nodded, remembering the list of notable people attending the Jubilee that Jennie had read out last night. Yes, there were dukes and duchesses, but there were also people who had made their marks in manufacturing and mining or who had won elections in lands like Canada or Australia.

"However," Holmes went on, "both in government and society, there are certain—*elements*, let us say—who do not approve of these reforms. I fear they are willing to sacrifice the Queen to achieve their ends."

"My friend Jacob used to live in Russia," Jennie said. "Some people tried to kill the emperor there—

the Czar. Jacob told me that the government undid all sorts of laws, taking back people's rights. That was why his parents left the country."

"I would like to believe such a thing could never happen here," Holmes said, returning to his search. "More important, I do not propose to allow the opportunity for these plotters to turn back the clock. Unfortunately, my efforts have been severely hampered these last few days. I did, however, learn that my captors plotted against the Queen's life, and now you add the information that a dynamite bomb is to be used. But as to when or, more important, *where* they intend to use it—"

"St. Ranulph's!" The words popped out of Wiggins's mouth.

Holmes turned to face Wiggins. "What's that?"

"Owens and I followed Limehouse Lew to St. Ranulph's," Wiggins elaborated. "He gave the key to the crypts to a posh bloke in a carriage. We didn't see who it was, but that same bloke later took the bomb from Limehouse—and then killed him."

"Today is the Jubilee parade, is it not?" Holmes asked.

"Yessir." Owens pulled out his battered copy of the *West Indian Advocate* he'd tucked back in his pocket that morning. "There's a map of the parade in here. We were going to be selling these, but—things happened."

Holmes snatched the newspaper from his hands. "Young man, if we succeed, this paper may be worth its weight in gold."

He all but tore the paper apart, looking for the map. Spreading it out on the chart table, he traced the route with his finger. "The parade will indeed pass St. Ranulph's Square."

Holmes's hand went to his waistcoat pocket, then fell away. "Those ruffians relieved me of my pocket watch." The detective glanced up at the sun from a porthole. "I judge that by now the parade has already begun."

Abruptly Holmes headed for the deck, beckoning his rescuers along. "First we must pass along a warning. Then it's off to St. Ranulph's, hopefully before the Queen arrives there!"

Chapter 17

WIGGINS COULDN'T FIGURE HOW HOLMES DID IT. The deck of the *Osiris* and the dock below were covered with police and their prisoners. Yet as Wiggins and his companions followed the detective back to dry land, the crowd parted before them.

Holmes marched straight for the highest-ranking police officer present, a tall inspector with ginger whiskers. The man's eyes went wide. "Good Lord! Mr. Holmes! I had no idea you were involved—"

"Very much so," Holmes replied. "These scoundrels were holding me prisoner aboard this vessel. The one with the broken nose admitted to a previous murder even as he was preparing to murder me."

Dooley stepped before the police official. "That's right. He killed my brother, Timothy Doolan—"

"A murder one of your policemen wouldn't do nothing about," Wiggins added.

"Will you make him pay for that now?" Dooley asked.

The inspector stood speechless.

"He will, young man. On that you have my word," Holmes told Dooley. He then turned back to the inspector. "But for now your greatest concern should be what else these fellows were up to. I believe they plan to attack the Queen."

The inspector's orangey red mustache seemed to uncurl and his face went pale. "Sir? What proof—?"

"You may be able to get something out of that ruffian with the broken nose, provided he awakens soon enough," Holmes said. "For myself, I'm going to St. Ranulph's Church, where I expect the assassin is lying in wait. Kindly provide that information to your superiors. They may wish to arrange a temporary delay in the procession to Hyde Park or perhaps a change of route."

The poor inspector's face was a sight to see. Scotland Yard had accepted Sherlock Holmes's advice on cases in the past, although police detectives took the credit when the solutions came out. However, there was not exactly a friendly spirit between the consulting detective and the police authorities.

To tell the Queen to halt her progress or even to change her course on the say-so of Sherlock Holmes . . .

Wiggins could tell that the inspector was worriedly considering the effect on his career from even passing Holmes's information along. On the other hand, if Holmes's warning turned out to be correct . . .

"The nearest telegraph office is approximately three intersections down that road." Holmes pointed impatiently. "You could offer some small assistance by accompanying me and flagging down that wagon approaching us."

Wiggins and his companions followed as Holmes led the mystified policeman to the roadway. The inspector raised his hand, commanding the wagon driver to stop.

The detective swooped up to the driver's perch behind the four-horse team, speaking quickly. In moments, the baffled-looking teamster, a bundle of pound notes in his hand, had joined the equally baffled-looking policeman down at the wharf side. Holmes now took up the reins.

"Hold hard there, Mr. Holmes!" Wiggins called, clambering aboard. "We're coming with you!"

"Yes, you might prove useful when we arrive."

Wiggins, Owens, Dooley, and Jennie barely had a chance to get settled atop the wagon's cargo before Holmes whipped up the horses. The wagon lurched forward, but Holmes still wasn't satisfied with their speed.

"Gee up!" he shouted, snapping the reins so they caught the horses with a solid *thwack!*

They were moving fast enough now to frighten Wiggins, who clung to the seat up beside Holmes. "The other traffic isn't moving as quickly as we are!" he said.

"Then they'd best get out of our path," Holmes replied. "Make way there!" he shouted. "We're on the Queen's business! Make way!"

Dumbfounded wagon drivers reined in at the spectacle of the tall gentleman driving the heavy wagon like a madman. A tinker on a donkey cart stopped his vehicle just short of colliding with the rushing wagon, sending curses after Holmes.

Now they were approaching the parade route, and they could see crowds ahead. Clinging to his perch, Wiggins got an idea. "That alley to the left will take us parallel to the parade." He risked his life to use one arm to point.

In spite of being bruised, unshaven, and gaunt, Holmes looked younger than Wiggins had ever seen him as he held those reins. The detective seemed to be enjoying himself. He actually glanced over at Wiggins with a grin. Wiggins's mouth fell open in shock. Had the great man *ever* grinned before?

They had managed to get within blocks of St. Ranulph's Square when the crush of people ahead forced Holmes to haul back on the reins and slow the wagon. Wiggins threw himself against the brake lever, and the wagon skidded to a stop.

The detective stared over the heads of the crowd at the steeple of the church rising to the sky. "It overlooks the line of march," he muttered, handing the reins to Wiggins. "You stay here and keep the wagon."

"Not bloody likely," Wiggins retorted. He came up with a couple of pennies and used them to hire a ragged street Arab to mind the wagon. Then he and the other members of the Raven League followed Holmes.

As they pressed through the crowd, they could see that all the faces were expectantly facing eastward. "The Queen hasn't yet arrived," Holmes declared. "You're sure the key was for the crypts?"

"That's what Limehouse said," Wiggins replied.

"Inconvenient," Holmes said. "One imagines that the conspirators would use the church spire as their observation post. But explosives in the crypt would bring down the church, spire and all."

"Maybe they're some kind of fanatics," Owens suggested.

"I don't think so." The detective shook his head. "However, these conspirators have shown themselves very willing to use any means to gain their ends." He glanced at the young members of the Raven League. "I'll start in the crypt. You can best spend your time informing any police in the vicinity of the situation."

"As if they'd listen to us," Owens muttered.

Wiggins watched Holmes snake his way through the crowd. "You know, he's pretty well done in," he said, concerned. "If he meets any more hard lads, he's going to need help." He turned to Jennie and Dooley.

Jennie was already shaking her head. "It's one thing to tell a constable that something suspicious is happening on a docked ship," she said. "It's another trying to convince one that the Queen is in danger."

"At least there's a chance of you getting them to listen. Dooley, you help her."

Wiggins didn't stay to argue. He pushed his way in the wake of Sherlock Holmes, Owens at his side.

Once upon a time, St. Ranulph's had been a country church, well outside of London. However, the city had expanded and swallowed up the parish. Some relics of the old days had survived. St. Ranulph's still had a tiny churchyard, where old gravestones stood at oddly tilted angles. They passed around the fenced-in area as they followed Mr. Holmes. The churchyard didn't offer much of a view, so the area was clear.

A set of steps to the side of the church entrance led down to the crypts. Holmes had already descended the stone stairway. He seemed to be fishing in the keyhole of the wooden door with a bit of wire. Shaking his head, he pulled out the wire and bent it into a new shape. With this attempt, he succeeded in making the lock release.

The boys arrived in time to help push open the door. Holmes peered into a sea of darkness cut only by the wedge of light coming from the door.

Propping the door open, Holmes entered, followed by the boys. They followed the sounds of muffled gasps and scraping until they discovered a bound figure left behind a pile of dusty caskets. It was an elderly man, dressed in a drab suit. His eyes bulged out at them over a handkerchief tied round his mouth.

"Thank heavens!" the man said hoarsely as Holmes ungagged him. "I thought no one could hear me!"

"You must be the verger," Holmes said. "I suppose it is your habit every morning to inspect the premises?"

"I come every morning, but when I arrived today, a pair of ruffians seized me and brought me down here. I told them I had no money, but all they wanted was my keys."

"Including the keys to the belfry above?" Holmes demanded.

"Yes, sir—they're all on the same ring."

Holmes looked at the boys. "Get this man free and bring him to the police immediately! I suspect my quarry awaits above. And this time, do not follow me!"

Wiggins and Owens set to work on the ropes that held the verger prisoner. They quickly had him free and on his feet.

"Do you think you can go find a copper—er, policeman—on your own, sir?" Owens asked as the verger blinked in the sunshine at the door. "Mr. Holmes may be getting into trouble, and we don't want to leave him alone."

Barely waiting for the man's response, the two boys dashed up the stairs leading to the church. Inside, they blinked in the sudden dimness. Holmes was nowhere to be seen, but they heard sounds overhead. They followed the faint noises to a stairway leading up into the spire. The boys looked at each other with no need to talk. They started up the stairs.

Six stories later, they reached the belfry—the open part of the tower where the bells rang out.

There they found Sherlock Holmes wrestling with a stranger.

The man fighting with the detective wasn't as tall as Holmes, but he was younger and definitely fresher. He broke loose and snatched up a small valise. As he did, the boys heard the sound of cheers coming from the crowd below.

Wiggins gasped. The Queen must be arriving!

Holmes must have heard as well. He charged at the assassin, trying to grapple with him again. Snarling, the man swung the valise, using it as a weapon. The force of the impact drove the detective back.

His blow did something else too. A loud ticking began to sound from inside the bag. He'd activated the dynamite bomb! The would-be assassin stared at the valise in sudden fear.

The momentary hesitation gave Holmes the chance to reel back into the fight. His opponent got ready to swing again, standing with his back to the boys. "Go for his left leg," Wiggins whispered to Owens. "I'll take the right!"

The two boys tackled the assassin just as he bashed at Holmes again. The detective went down—but so did the assassin.

Cursing, the man clouted Wiggins with his fist, knocking him off his leg. Then he used his free leg to kick Owens in the ribs. With a cry of pain, Owens lost his grip. The assassin rose to his knees, turning to the large opening that overlooked the street. Wiggins got a glimpse of a street full of red uniforms. One toss and the bomb would go down to the Queen and the crowd below—including Jennie and Dooley.

Wiggins shook his head and came at the man again. This time he wrapped his arms around the valise.

"Stupid brat!" the assassin growled. "Any second now, this thing goes up under you!"

Wiggins tried to fasten his teeth in the man's wrist, but his opponent grabbed him by the hair. Using his superior strength, the man peeled Wiggins loose.

Before he could throw the infernal device, Sherlock Holmes lurched at him, managing to spin the assassin around. The valise flew loose, soaring in the opposite direction. It tumbled to the floor at the far side of the belfry, beneath an opening over the empty churchyard.

The assassin crashed into a nearby wall. Holmes and Wiggins converged on him. "You've failed," the detective said. "The whole plot is coming apart. We know that bomb came from a group of London criminals. Now we need to know who sent you."

His back to the opening, the would-be bomber stood panting before them. "They got a long reach," he said. "If I talk, they'd do for me, my family, and all . . . and it won't be pretty."

Head down, he made a furious lunge for the bomb. But before he could reach it, Owens scooped it up and flung it over the ledge, down into the churchyard— away from the street. Holding one hand to his injured ribs, Owens stood there, one fist curled, daring the assassin to do his worst.

Instead, the man did something no one expected— he threw himself after the bomb.

Holmes leaped forward, grabbing the man's wrist, but only for a moment. The weakened detective couldn't maintain the hold, and the man dropped free.

The assassin screamed as he fell, but his cries were lost in the explosion from below. The whole spire seemed to totter, and for a horrible moment Wiggins thought it was going over. But the structure stood, and Holmes and the boys rushed to the opening.

A large, smoking crater stood in the midst of the churchyard. The tilted gravestones were now knocked flat. As for the assassin, Wiggins could see no trace of him.

The sound of heavy boots clattering up the belfry stairs turned them around. A squad of red-coated soldiers burst in, their rifles at the ready.

An officer with a pistol in his hand stared at them. "Mr. Holmes?" he said. "We were sent ahead after the Queen received your warning." He glanced at the boys. "Where is the perpetrator of this outrage?"

Holmes put a shaky hand on Wiggins's and Owens's shoulders. "These young men assisted in foiling the plot," he declared. "As for the perpetrator, he followed his infernal device—no doubt to the infernal regions." Under his breath, the detective added, "Taking his secrets with him."

Satisfied that the situation in the belfry was under control, the army officer went to the opening over the street and gave a hand signal. Holmes and the boys joined him. Down in the roadway below, the police had restored order. The procession was already starting up again.

A somewhat reduced cavalry escort passed below, then the gilded coach with Queen Victoria. As the monarch of all Britain passed them, she gave a regal wave to her defenders in the belfry.

Holmes, Owens, and Wiggins responded with their best bows.

Chapter 18

THE ASSASSINATION ATTEMPT SANK ALMOST WITHOUT a ripple in the other excitement surrounding the Queen's Jubilee. Wiggins heard no newsboys crying up the story, and although Jennie managed to get hold of several newspapers, she only found a single paragraph about an explosion along the route of the procession.

"You'd think *that* would be news," she said a little huffily.

"My mama's cousin says there's a lot of news that happens but never gets printed up," Owens said.

"Mr. Holmes said that this wasn't the first time somebody tried to do in Her Majesty," Wiggins said. "Maybe they don't write about it to keep other geezers from getting ideas."

He glanced at Jennie. "Y'know, Dr. Watson some-times writes stories and keeps them in a box for the future."

"Humph," Jennie said. "Maybe I'll do that with this one."

Wiggins kicked at the pavement, feeling strange and uncomfortable in a new pair of shoes. They were supposed to fit perfectly, but his feet were used to ex-tra wrapping and padding.

Both Wiggins and Owens stood awkwardly in new suits of clothes that had arrived at their homes the day before. Jennie also wore a new outfit, but she seemed more at home in good clothing.

That's about all she has, Wiggins realized. *Everything else she and her mother brought to London must have been lost in the fire.*

A four-wheeled carriage came round the corner. Wiggins had expected a cab, but this rig was much more elegant.

It was definitely for them, however. Dooley's head poked out one window, a huge grin all but splitting the boy's face.

They soon joined him inside the carriage, Owens and Wiggins sitting opposite from Dr. Watson and Sherlock Holmes while Jennie took a seat beside the adults.

"I feared we might be delayed," Holmes said. "I was called away by business with my brother, Mycroft."

Maybe it was the thought of Holmes's business or perhaps the mention of a brother, but Dooley asked, "Have they found out anything more about that broke-nosed bloke who killed Tim?"

"The strange death of Mr. Rowley was one of the things Mycroft wanted to discuss with Holmes, I believe," Watson said.

"The broken-nosed thug has been identified as Bruiser Rowley," Holmes said. "In spite of being kept in the most secure cell in Scotland Yard under constant guard, he was found with a look of terror on his face, dead from a broken neck."

"Now we'll never know who his boss was," Owens said.

"That was a man who deserved to hang for what he did to Tim." Dooley shook his head. "I can't help feeling he cheated us, dying like that."

Wiggins, however, couldn't help but remember the words of the would-be assassin before he flung himself to his death. *They*, whoever they were, certainly *did* have a long reach.

The carriage arrived at Paddington Station, and Holmes donned an elegant silk hat. "I thought we'd be seeing your new deerstalker cap for a trip to the country," Wiggins said, gesturing to the silk hat Holmes held.

"Ah," the detective replied, "perhaps another day."

"Where are we going, Mr. Holmes?" Jennie asked. The only response was a faint smile.

The mystery deepened as Holmes and Watson led their young companions up to a platform without buying a ticket. A uniformed attendant immediately conveyed them to a coach.

"Wherever we're going, there ain't all that many others going there," Dooley commented, glancing around the almost-deserted platform.

Inside, instead of a series of compartments, they found themselves in what looked like a parlor, taking up half of the railway carriage.

"Blimey!" Owens said. "This is more posh than your house, Mr. H."

The overstuffed chairs and other furniture

would have been enough to furnish rooms for all the children's families. Jennie hesitantly tested the upholstery on the couch that ran under one window. "We had third-class seats on the train coming down from Tollton," she said, "and Mother thought they were frightfully dear. This must be first class. I'm afraid to think what the tickets must cost."

Holmes and Watson had the young people sit down, and within moments, the train smoothly pulled away from the platform without even a lurch.

Dooley, Jennie, and Owens took places by the windows, commenting on the cityscape passing outside. When Wiggins looked out, he noticed there were fewer houses and the train was steaming past a suburban station. What kind of a train was this that didn't make any stops? Where exactly were they going?

Before Wiggins could question his hosts, however, Dr. Watson produced a notebook and began asking the members of the Raven League about the recently concluded case. After getting several details from his guests, Watson turned to Wiggins. "You risked yourself on a number of occasions for your friends."

"He didn't want it to happen again," Dooley said.

"Didn't want what to happen?" Holmes asked.

"What happened to my brother," Dooley said in a small voice.

Slowly, after much questioning, the detective and his doctor friend put together the full story of what had happened to Tim Doolan and how Wiggins had been unable to face it, even if it meant the end of the Baker Street Irregulars.

Small red spots appeared in Holmes's cheeks, and his voice grew loud. "I fail to understand why you didn't come to me," he said. "Your young friend came to grief following something he thought to be my business. You should—"

Dr. Watson gently put a hand on his friend's forearm. "Should he have any clue as to how you would react based on your earlier dealings with the Irregulars?" Watson asked.

"I should think—I imagine—" Holmes's expression grew less sharp and more thoughtful. "I expect you are correct, Watson," he said quietly. Then he turned to Wiggins. "However, after our recent experiences, I trust you will be able to come to me with any problems in future."

Wiggins didn't know what to say, so he was glad for the distraction when a lavishly dressed gentleman knocked at the door to the carriage and entered. "Your presence is desired," he announced.

Wiggins looked the man over. Running errands had brought him into contact with footmen and butlers at the houses of wealthy people. He'd never heard of servants on trains. And from the way this geezer was dressed, he would look more proper as the owner of some of those grand houses rather than a servant.

Holmes, Watson, and the children followed the elegant man through several elaborately furnished carriages. Then he opened a door, and a voice inside announced, "Mr. Sherlock Holmes, Dr. Watson, and . . . companions."

They entered a large railway car with a number of people standing and one person sitting in a large, almost thronelike chair.

That seemed only appropriate. The seated person was Queen Victoria.

Wiggins felt his eyes going wide. The Queen looked smaller than he expected—older too than the image on Owens's medal. She was a little, plump person in her sixties with a round, plain face under a white cap. But as she straightened in her chair, she looked every inch the queen.

Holmes and Watson stepped forward and gave her deep bows. Taking the cue, Wiggins, Owens, and Dooley did the same, while Jennie dropped into a curtsy.

The Queen gestured for them to rise. "We understand that you were all instrumental in foiling a plot against our person," she said.

"It was an honor for us to serve Your Majesty," Holmes replied.

"That service was also accomplished at considerable peril to yourselves," the Queen observed. "We wish to offer some small token of our thanks."

Another functionary in elegant court dress appeared by the chair, opening a leather case. Small gold items gleamed against the velvet lining.

"We were further informed that the young persons involved in this affair organized themselves into a Raven League," the Queen said, "based, no doubt on the belief that so long as the ravens live within the Tower of London, the Empire will stand."

"An' Mr. Pilbeam—" Dooley started, until

Wiggins gave him a discreet elbow in the ribs. The Queen did not need to hear that they had named their group after a pub.

Instead, Wiggins said, "Mr. Pilbeam served as a Yeoman Warder at the Tower, ma'am. He told us all about the ravens."

The Queen nodded and beckoned Holmes and Watson forward. She presented each of them with a long tiepin decorated with a gold raven. The young people had smaller raven pins fixed to their lapels. Wiggins held his breath, afraid his chest would burst with pride. He made his best bow to the Queen.

"I wish my father could see this," Owens whispered to Jennie. "I bet this would make him proud of me."

"I'd guess he already is," she replied.

"Go now," Queen Victoria said, raising her hand in salute. "With our thanks."

Holmes bowed. "Your Majesty, your recognition alone is thanks enough."

He stepped back, gently shepherding his young companions with him. They were nearly out the door when a voice rose above the gentle hubbub.

It wasn't loud, and Wiggins wasn't even sure where it came from. But it sounded clearly in his ears.

". . . don't understand why the Court should deal with such ragamuffins."

The pride inflated within Wiggins's chest burst like a balloon stabbed with a sharp icicle. Around him, he could feel Jennie, Dooley, and Owens flinch as well.

Then the Queen spoke into the sudden, dead silence that filled the room. "Why should we deal with them? Because, sir, they are our loyal subjects and Britain's future."

Preceding Holmes and Watson, Wiggins and his friends left the royal presence, their backs straight and heads held high.

Whatever might come, the Raven League was ready to face it.